Swan

and the

Bear

Furry United Coalition #2

Eve Langlais

New York Times Bestseller

Copyright © December 2011, Eve Langlais
Cover Art by Amanda Kelsey © December 2011
Edited by Brieanna Robertson
Produced in Canada

Published by Eve Langlais
Published by Eve Langlais
1606 Main Street, PO Box 151,
Stittsville, Ontario, Canada, K2S1A3
www.EveLanglais.com

ISBN-13: 978-1537249773
ISBN-10: 1537249770

ALL RIGHTS RESERVED

Prologue

The heat from the inferno, fed on chemicals and years of hard work, singed whiskers and dried exposed skin, sucking the moisture from the air and leaving the mouth dry. The acrid stench of smoke made a tickle form in twitching nostrils, but determination held the sneeze at bay. Nothing, however, could halt the fire, which devoured everything in its path.

Ruined! Everything is ruined.

And things were progressing so well. The elusive chemical cocktail that would make even the puniest of shifters into creatures worth respecting was so close to completion. *Ah to finally be a monster with big freakn' teeth!* The dream of a lifetime gone up in smoke.

Gnashing tiny, pointed teeth wasn't anywhere close to satisfying, but frustrated, it proved the only available outlet to relieve some of the tension. What would have really made the moment bearable was going rabid on the person responsible. The blame for this fiasco resided on the shoulders of one irritatingly bubbly bunny. Because of the fluffy monstrosity, and her friends at FUC, the project of a lifetime went from almost smashing success to burning failure.

So unfair! And reminiscent of the days on the schoolyard when the popular group would lord it over the less fortunate, their genetic perfection making everything fall with ease in their laps. No more. Time to level the playing field through scientific manipulation and get revenge on those who thought to stand in the way of success, starting with one irritating cotton-tailed female! Miranda would pay, she and everyone else who'd contributed to destroying the Frankenstein lab—*my pride and joy*—with its bevy of special creations.

Thankfully, they'd never found the lab mockingly named Moreau with its secret scientific installation—and cages full of failures. From the ashes of defeat, the rebuilding would begin, success would finally be achieved, and revenge maliciously plotted.

I'll kill you, Miranda, you and that big brown bear you call mate! Then, I'll take on the world.

Muah-*cough*-erk. Bleh. Damned smoke.

Chapter One

Mason tried to fight it, he truly did, but bears ever did have one ultimate failing—curiosity. In his case, he also had impulse control issues. His poor mother often lamented the fact he acted before thinking as she paddled his bottom. Mason preferred to think of his antics as refreshing, spontaneous, and fun. Needless to say, he'd gotten in trouble a lot as a cub, and still did as an adult.

Case in point, the dilemma before him. He knew he should walk away. *This is such a bad idea.* His inner conscience truly did try to warn him, but...

The temptation proved too hard to resist, especially with it wagging right in front of him. Encased in what looked like men's cargo pants stretched taut around a full-bottomed behind, it begged for it. He could almost hear it screaming, "Do it!"

Mason wound up and smacked the bobbing ass. Unfortunately, the outcome wasn't exactly how he pictured it. In his experience, when he complimented a butt, the female squealed, pretended affront, then came on to him with lashes batting in delight.

Not in this case.

The woman, hidden under the desk, reared up with a startled shriek, whacked her head, and let out a stream of curses that would have made most sailors blush. However, since Mason had used all the expressions at one time or another, he didn't even blink. Although, he did take a step back when the owner of the slapped ass started detailing in vivid oral elegance what she would do to him when she got her hands on him.

Shuffling back while still hunched over, the object of his attention cleared the desk and stood, flipping as she did a silky mane of dark hair that tickled the skin of his face as it swept by. But he didn't mind once he got a look at her.

Happy birthday to me. Despite her potty mouth—which could do delightfully dirty things to him anytime it liked—he beheld feminine perfection with a few extra curves—*more cushion for the pushing.* Reaching his chin, the wearer of the cargo pants had ebony skin, which gleamed like the richest of chocolates. Round cheeks, full red lips, a snub nose and dark, really annoyed eyes greeted him. As if that weren't enough, Ms. Hot-Ass possessed the most fascinating hair—long and feathered in layers, black as sin but tipped in white, even the edges of her bangs. It gave her an exotic look he found quite appealing. Just ask his twitching cock.

Inhaling, he took a sniff and his toes curled in delight at the spicy citrus scent that emanated from her. He did so like his fruit, especially the eating part. Further examination of his whiff and he determined she belonged to the bird genome, although he couldn't quite pinpoint which caste. Not that he cared. Unlike his snobby brother, Mason enjoyed the ladies of all species, because as everyone knew, bears loved their *honey.* Mix it with some sweet pussy pie, and they were in heaven.

His mouth already watering at her imagined taste, he smiled at the angry woman—a thousand watt, panty-dropping whopper of a grin—and waited for her scowl to melt along with her inhibitions.

Unlikely as it seemed, her glare deepened until her eyes shot veritable daggers at him, dozens of sharp, pointed objects with unerring aim that almost made him flinch and definitely dampened his cheerful mug.

Faced with such antagonism, he decided to rely on his charm. With a voice women called velvet seduction, he said, "Hi. How you doing?" Okay, so he borrowed—ahem, stole—that line from Joey off the show *Friends*. How could he resist? The man was pure genius when it came to getting women.

Even that didn't work on the steaming mad hottie. She planted her hands on her hips—nicely curved ones made for gripping—and curled her lip disdainfully. "I was doing fine until you came in. You'd better have a good excuse for slapping my butt, Mason Brownsmith, or you're going to find yourself one day, real soon, in a cell full of convicts who are going to find your ass mighty interesting."

As threats went, it was pretty damned good, and frightening if she meant it. "Darling, you wound me. I was just complimenting you on your fabulous buttocks. I promise, hard as the temptation will be, to keep my hands to myself from now on, unless you want them on you." He raised a hopeful brow. She shot it down with an arched one of her own. Damn, but that just made her more desirable. "It seems you have me at a disadvantage. You know my name and all I know about you is that I'd like to get to know you better." He left out the naked part. Somehow, he didn't think she'd appreciate it. Yet. Optimism—one of his finer traits.

"I'm Jessie Cygnclair, FUC agent and head of the technical department, and totally unimpressed with your feeble attempt to get in my pants. I don't sleep with coworkers. I don't find crass sexual come-ons sexy, and I most definitely have no intention of getting to know you, a proven manwhore, better."

Mason slapped a hand over his heart in mock injury, not entirely untrue given the blow to his ego. "Manwhore? That's harsh. I prefer the term erotic specialist with a degree in oral pleasure." He waggled his lips in opposing directions—a hit with the ladies, especially once they got their pants off—and winked.

Unimpressed, she kicked him, hard, in the shin.

"Ow!" He hopped on one foot and thanked his stars she'd not aimed higher. She wore black combat boots with what felt like steel enforced toes.

"Get out." Not an ounce of sympathy entered her expression as she crossed her arms under an impressive set of tits.

"But—"

"Out," she snarled. "And if you come back, I won't be responsible for the consequences."

Seeing as how he was apparently off his game, Mason thought it better to retreat and regroup. He slunk out with his short bear tail tucked between his legs. That only lasted until he hit the hall and his confidence came seeping back. So what if one mocha-skinned tech geek didn't think he was God's gift to women? She'd eventually get the memo, and when she came begging and smiling…he'd make her scream in pleasure, of course. He never could hold grudges, especially not where beautiful women were concerned.

Now, back to his current mission—finding his office. His temporary one. The undercover department he worked for—so secret even most shifters didn't know it existed—had decided that with his cover as a benign lawyer blown, there was no point in not letting FUC make use of his services.

For the uninformed, FUC stood for the Furry United Coalition. Personally, Mason preferred the original title that included defense at the end, but the tight asses in power decided FUCD crossed the line. A shame. The fun he could have had with announcing he was FUCD were endless.

No matter the name, the agency provided a police service of sorts for other shape-shifters like himself. Well, the furry ones on land anyway. The birds and water dwellers preferred to have their own agencies, a bit of species racism that Mason didn't understand. But despite the lines drawn between their kind, they often worked together on cases that crossed over. They even traded agents back and forth with specialties that were needed.

Mason himself once volunteered to help the Mer-alliance, as the merfolk called themselves. Wearing a diving suit and a breathing apparatus hadn't impeded his ability at all to see just what mermaids hid under their tails. It should be noted that those belonging to the shark pool, though, had teeth. Talk about a close call. It did explain why the ratio of males to females, though, was so vast.

Despite his volunteer work underwater, he'd never openly worked for FUC before. As a special ops agent, he usually worked as an undercover operative for the shifter government going wherever they sent him to spy, spreading his love around and gathering information—among other things.

Unlike his older brother, who used to take the term chaste to the extreme, Mason saw no problem with bringing pleasure to the opposite sex. Although, since his last mission, things back home had changed. Mason returned to find his brother hooked up with some hot ass, buxom blonde. Brave man considering his mate turned into a freakn' saber-toothed bunny. And no, that wasn't a joke. Mason might have seen plenty of messed up things in his career, but, for some reason, a slavering, enormous, fluffy white bunny with red eyes and foot long fangs gave him the heebie-jeebies.

Miranda's special bunny side was the reason both she and his brother were recently in mortal danger, a danger Mason almost single-handedly resolved. Him and a handful of well-placed plastic charges that was. What a shame he'd forgotten to bring marshmallows when they'd gone off in an explosion of epic proportions. The laboratory housing the evil mastermind behind the plot to kidnap and experiment on shifters went *kaboom* in a great big ball of fire. Just in time, too, because human Marines arrived within hours to thankfully only discover glowing coals and ashes.

Mason had kept the secret of shifters safe from the humans. Yes, the term hero applied, and he'd make sure to use it often when he hit the bar tonight looking for some fun.

Thinking back to the recent case again, though, the information they'd netted on their raid proved invaluable. FUC, along with his special ops group, ended up taking down three other testing facilities and saving a few shifters, those that weren't irrevocably damaged. Others found in the cells and cages were dying or stark raving mad from the experimentation done to them in the medical facilities, a tragic reminder that not all nightmares ended when the mastermind's reign of terror did.

Unfortunately, the recent operation had an unfortunate side effect with his superiors discovering Mason's cover as a secret operative was blown, making his days as a spy over. Switching up his job to make him a field liaison to FUC, they'd added desk duty as part of his new obligations. *Sob.* A bear of action, Mason belonged out in the field, scaling walls, breaking into secure installations, stealing picnic baskets. Okay, the latter he did just for fun.

But at least he no longer had to work at his brother's boring law firm pretending he knew what the hell he did. More than one divorce case ended up going the wife's way under his inexperienced hands, to the chagrin of his male clients. Oops. The divorce and probate world probably breathed a sigh of relief when he got reassigned to the local FUC division.

"Mason!" His new boss's bark made him pivot. Kloe craned her long neck in his direction and tilted her head toward an open door. Then she disappeared inside and didn't wait to see if he followed. She just assumed. God, he loved bossy women. Too bad the leggy giraffe was already taken. He wouldn't have minded tapping that. Although, not as much as he wanted to tap that sweet piece of chocolate with the feisty temper.

Striding into his new boss's office, he flung

himself into a seat and grinned at her with all the white-toothed charm of a boy scout selling cookies.

It worked, with Kloe beaming back, proving he'd not lost his touch. What a relief.

"Rascal. I hear you're already making trouble."

"Just saying hello to my fellow coworkers," he replied innocently.

"Say hello with your mouth next time instead of your hand."

"Mouth. Gotcha," he agreed, winking suggestively.

Kloe sighed. "I can see you're going to be a handful."

He couldn't resist saying it, even if she was his boss. "Actually, I'm more like two."

Kloe gaped at him before giving her head a shake. "Oh, you're going to make things interesting around here. Let me ask you, how did your superiors punish you when you drove the females in your division nuts?"

"Laps around the training complex, chin-ups, and pushups, ma'am. It's how I got this body." He flexed an impressive arm and grinned. And it should be noted, that women didn't usually complain about his advances. On the contrary, they tended to seduce him. The punishment came because of the other males complaining. *Is it my fault woman love me?*

"That might explain the body, but what about his fat head?" added a familiar sultry yet grumpy voice.

"I knew you couldn't resist me," he taunted, craning in his seat to see the yummy Jessie stride into the office.

"I can't resist buying chips and dip either. It still doesn't mean it's healthy. Now, if you're done making crude jokes that make me want to petition for a sexual harassment free workplace, I have news of import. It concerns your brother and Miranda."

His joking mien immediately sobered. "Report."

She appeared taken aback by his change in persona. He'd played the role of irreverent playbear for so long, he'd forgotten that most people didn't realize it was an act, an act he enjoyed most of the time.

"I've been deciphering some more of the coded information on that hard drive you guys snagged from that complex. Most of it is self-destructing as I extract it, but I did salvage enough pieces to surmise it's doubtful the mastermind behind the abductions and experimentation died in the fire."

"Like hell. That place was hot enough to melt freaking steel," Mason interjected. "Nothing could have survived."

Jessie made a buzzer sound. "Wrong!"

"What makes you think that, Jessie?" Kloe asked, leaning forward and holding out her hand for the printouts clutched in Jessie's fist.

Jessie handed them over then folded her hands over her stomach as she told them what she knew. "According to a fragment of an email discussing emergency evacuation should the facility come under attack, there were exit tunnels built into the place at key points. According to the depositions of Mr. Brownsmith and other operatives, it was believed from the words and actions of the enemy force that the person running the show was holed up in an office, which was, of course, located right over one of those escape tunnels."

"We saw no trace of those even after the fire died down," he replied with a frown. "Are you sure?"

The look she gave him spoke quite eloquently what she thought of his doubtful tone. "Very sure. If escape became necessary, there were traps in place to cave in the entrances hiding their existence. It's really quite clever. But back to my main reason for interrupting, with the mastermind possibly still on the loose, unlike previously thought, it means there is a large chance that Miranda, and by default, your brother, are once again in danger. This sicko was after her blood because of her saber-tooth tendency. It is my recommendation that they be put under guard along with her immediate family."

"And what about everyone else?" Mason asked quietly. "Miranda and her folks weren't the only ones they were after. I saw some of their test subjects. People, normal shifters, whose only crime was existing. How do we protect them?" Their eyes still haunted him along with their pleas to end their suffering. No one should ever have to go through what they had. Not to mention, his kind couldn't take that kind of loss without it impacting the population.

The shifter community, while spread all over the world, didn't exist in vast numbers. Their birth rates tended toward the low side and they courted higher fatality rates than humans. Certain genomes, like the wolves and big cats, thrived for the most part, but never became too large as a group because of their violent tendencies. The weaker castes, like birds, bunnies—normal ones unlike Miranda—and rodents often ended up as lunch when they shifted out in the wild—regular hawks didn't care if the mouse they ingested was a professor for a local college. Add in humans on the hunt for them—those that knew their secret, and those that just saw a trophy—intergroup jostling for power along with a sick mastermind, and their kind could very well end up on the extinct species list. Heck, the panda shifters were almost there. It made protecting those that remained so important, a mission Mason gladly undertook. Not that he said all that aloud. People tended to laugh when he did, the curse of a playbear role played too well. But faced with a serious brown gaze, a gaze that took his measure—and found him wanting—he wished for once he could prove there was more to the bear than met the eye. He tried to relay some of his inner thoughts as he met Jessie's stare, sober as a judge.

Jessie blinked, a puzzled crease forming between her brows. "I'm sorry, but we can't protect everyone. We can only try and guess as to what the sicko might do next."

"She's right, Mason," said Kloe, her voice low with regret. "Much as I'd love to give everyone in the community a guard, it just isn't feasible. But, there might be a way we can use this information to trap the mastermind. Until this moment, we believed him dead. What if we released information to the community stating our certainty of it? If the mastermind thinks he can act without anyone to stop him, he might get sloppy and fall right into our laps."

"Chase won't like it."

"Like Miranda will let him make that decision for her," snorted Jessie. "You have met her, right?"

Mason shuddered. Had he ever. He'd take a

raging bull instead any day. "Good point. But still…"

"I don't see as how we've got any other options at the moment. We've got no clues other than those hidden on the few hard drives we recovered."

"And I'm working on those as fast as I can, in between other duties," Jessie added rather defensively.

"I never said you weren't," Kloe replied. "But for all we know, they're a waste of time because we can't be sure there's any info of import to be found on them. It could be that using Miranda as bait is our best bet to luring the mastermind out into the open."

Much as Mason hated to admit it, Kloe was probably right. The mastermind had hidden from them for years now. If it hadn't been for the shifter abductions—a population already small in numbers—and the recovery of medically tortured bodies, they might have never known he even existed. Shifters went missing all the time, usually victims of nature. Discovering that someone intentionally killed their kind as part of some sick project… It blew, large. Forewarned that the madness might start again, they could work to make sure the mastermind didn't have time to regroup and restart his disgusting project.

However, knowing his brother's feelings for his new mate, Mason wondered how he'd feel dangling his bunny out in the open like a tasty carrot. *And lucky me, they must have decided I'm expendable seeing as how they expect me to broach it with my temperamental sibling.* Thankfully, his last will and testament was already in order.

Chapter Two

The door whipped open within seconds of his knock to reveal a bright smile and a freckled nose—his new sister-in-law and a danger to society. Mason immediately thrust the bakery box into Miranda's arms.

"It's carrot cake, extra icing," he said quickly before she turned all furry and toothy on him. The first time they'd met a few days before, he'd gotten caught as he raided his brother's fridge, and to add insult to injury, interrupted Miranda's morning nookie plans. The double whammy saw him stuffed into a closet and gagged with his own sock. That part wasn't so bad, it was listening to his brother and mate go at it—quite vocally—that probably scarred him for life.

"Aren't you just the sweetest?" Miranda exclaimed, somehow managing to balance the cake with one hand while she threw herself at him for a hug. Soft curves pressed against him and Mason relaxed as the chances of death by rabid bunny receded. Then shot right back up again as he saw Chase glaring at him over Miranda's shoulders.

He extricated himself, not easy seeing as how Miranda seemed to have some anaconda mixed into her bloodline somewhere down the line. Her grip on his arm as she yanked him into the apartment proved quite firm and unbreakable.

"Honey bear, look who came to visit."

"I'm not blind," retorted his brother dryly.

Not that Miranda, beaming like the world's blondest Barbie and escaped mental patient, cared. She shoved Mason in the direction of the couch and hopped off to the kitchen, probably to stuff her face with cake. Mason wisely kept that observation to himself. No need to antagonize the furry killer.

"Speak quickly. Dinner is almost ready." Chase, seated across from him, crossed his arms over his massive chest. Irritable, glowering, and unafraid to show it, at least some things, like his brother's sunny personality, never changed.

Taking a deep breath to speak, Mason just about drooled instead when his brain caught up to what the savory aroma meant. "Mmm, is that pot roast, potatoes, honey glazed carrots, and fresh bread I smell?"

"Yes. And there's not enough for you."

"Aw, come on, just a little," Mason begged. He'd not enjoyed some of his brother's special roast—their mama's recipe—in months now.

"No."

"Oh grumpy one," Miranda hollered from the kitchen. "Remember what I said about sharing, especially with family. This will be great practice for when we go see my parents next week."

"But I don't want to go visit."

"Then you can kiss your honey pie privileges goodbye," she threatened.

A tic formed in Chase's cheek and his brows beetled together. Through a jaw stiff enough to give granite a run for its money, he said, "Would you like to stay for dinner?" Chase's eyes declared death if he did.

"I'd love to," Mason said with a grin, crooking his finger at his brother in a come-and-get-me gesture.

Chase would have probably snapped and taken him up on the offer too, but Miranda came bouncing out of nowhere and landed on her mate's lap, all five feet nothing of curves and blonde, curly hair.

"What's up, doc?" she asked, her expression serious even if her green eyes danced with mirth.

Chase snorted. "Have you been watching Bugs Bunny again?"

"Maybe a little. Just trying to stay true to my roots, you know, especially with junior fluffball possibly on the way."

"We've only be sleeping together for just over two weeks. You are not pregnant." Chase stated this as a fact, but as a male, Mason caught the glimpse of fear in his eyes. *Sucker!* Oh how the big and ornery had fallen.

"Yet," she corrected. "I don't think you're trying hard enough."

"Oh I'll give it to you hard." Chase's promise came out low and growly.

"Promise?" Miranda replied, batting her lashes.

Mason gagged. "Oh gross. Excuse me for interrupting your foreplay, but in case you hadn't noticed, there's a little brother sitting right here."

A chuckle rumbled forth from his older sibling. "Oh that's priceless coming from you, the family manwhore."

"Hey, what is it with people calling me that today?"

"Ooh, who else called you a slut?" Miranda asked, eyes wide with interest.

"Jessie over at the FUC offices did after I complimented her ass. But in my defense, I think I was off my game."

Miranda snorted. "Ha. Not likely. Jessie's one tough cookie. She's all about work, no play. I keep telling her to indulge in a good boink to lighten up, but she claims she's got better things to do with those thirty seconds of her life than watch some guy sweat and grunt."

Mason winced. Thirty seconds? He'd have a bad attitude about sex too with that kind of experience. "So she's not dating anyone right now, I take it?" He tried not to sound like he cared about the answer, and failed miserably judging by the twitch of Miranda's nose.

"Ooh, someone's interested in Jessie." Miranda just about sang the words as she bounced on her mate's lap.

"And someone here doesn't care," Chase grumbled. "Can we get off the topic of Jessie and her sex life? Somehow, I don't think she'd like it."

"No, she wouldn't, and she can do evil things to get even," Miranda whispered.

"Why are you whispering?" Mason asked.

Miranda cast a suspicious eye around her. "When I was protecting Chase, we had cameras installed to keep an eye on him. They're supposed to be deactivated."

The implication made Mason laugh. "I'm sure they still are. Knowing what you guys like to do, she'd have gone blind by now or torn her own eyes out watching the pair of you go at it."

"I think someone's jealous," Chase said smugly.

Jealous that his brother found a woman who loved to have lots of sex and made him happy? One woman? The same woman for the rest of his life? The answer should have been a resounding no. Wasn't his motto something along the lines that variety was the spice of life? But, seeing Miranda snuggled on Chase's lap, his grumpy older brother actually smiling, his face soft and intimate as he whispered something in her ear, a pang of envy struck Mason. What would it feel like to have one person always be there for him? Someone he could share secrets, crack jokes, make sweet love to everyday… Oddly enough, a flash of chocolate brown eyes and a cocky smirk came to mind. He shook his head. *It seems my brother's madness is contagious.*

No way was Mason ready to settle down. He liked the single life of a playbear. "So, what are we doing first? Having dinner or talking about the FUC plan to use Miranda as bait?"

Yeah, that little announcement saw Chase setting Miranda aside so he could tackle Mason to the floor and use his head as a hammer. Mason freely admitted to himself that he used his startling news to distract his mind and body from a certain mocha-skinned hottie. It worked, too, until the envy returned when Miranda kissed Chase's booboos better. Mason's throbbing jaw, though, didn't get the same kind of treatment, which kind of bummed him out. *Why can't I have someone kiss me all better too?*

Why not indeed?

* * * *

Jessie snorted in disgust, mostly with herself, for watching the unfolding drama. *I am such a heel for listening in on the conversation between Miranda, Chase, and that pain in my ass, Mason.* Miranda would have kicked her butt from one end of the building to the other if she knew Jessie had reactivated the cameras just to have a fly on the wall presence when Mason dropped his bombshell.

Lying to herself, she came up with the excuse that she did it to make sure Mason didn't pussy out, but truthfully, she couldn't deny a certain morbid curiosity in the bear. Sure, she knew of his reputation as a ladies man, an impression reinforced with his actions. But still, he fascinated her on a level she didn't understand.

The earlier ass slap admittedly took her by surprise, but not because she didn't enjoy it like she'd pretended, more because no one had ever before dared to smack her butt. Ex-boyfriends certainly hadn't, and she always assumed the fault lay with her because they found her butt too big, the term bubble coming to mind. She couldn't deny a certain amount of pleasure knowing someone found it hot enough to slap. Of course, the fact that the hand involving in the smack belonged to a proven manwhore took some of the enjoyment away, because he probably tapped anything in sight.

But knowing that didn't stop her from experiencing a girlish tingle from head to toe—and in between—when she beheld him in person, his cocky grin sending moisture to parts that usually required lube. The pictures she saw hadn't done him justice.

Tall, wide, and muscled—so thickly, deliciously muscled. The cords of his thighs stretched denim, the bulges of his biceps strained his t-shirt, and a glance down showed his feet were freaking huge, which went well with his massive hands. It also made her wonder if the old wives tales were true...

As if that weren't enough, he possessed the chiseled face of a god with a square chin, strong nose, and a set of lips that quirked into the most amazing smile ever. And he knew it too, the bastard.

Despite the activity in her undies, she refused to give in to his charm because that was all it was. She owned an X chromosome. He possessed a Y. Nature dictated he try to get in her pants. He hit on her because flirting in his world came as natural as breathing.

And yet, he fascinated her. After their meeting in Kloe's office, she'd done some research and discovered most of his files were classified. Not that it stopped her from digging deeper and hitting even more dead ends. What she did glean was he'd served the shifter community well during his years undercover. He owned several commendations and came with high praise from his superiors.

But she learned nothing of the man himself, well, other than he didn't have a steady girlfriend and wore a size fourteen shoe. So, yes, she spied on him, activating the cameras she'd not had the time to remove from Chase and Miranda's apartment. She only cursed a minor blue streak when she heard herself mentioned. Made a moue of displeasure when Miranda revealed her thoughts on sex. Then flushed with guilt when they discussed the fact she might be watching.

This is why they say it's never good to eavesdrop. Hearing people speak frankly always hurt even if they spoke only the truth. It didn't stop her from watching, though, as Chase and Mason tussled, Chase winning only because Mason didn't employ any of the moves he'd learned while in the service, a nice brotherly gesture that made her frown. She'd expected, wrongly apparently, that he'd try to win at any cost.

With the fight over, they sat down to talk and eat, mostly a recap of what Jessie had briefed them on earlier while in Kloe's office.

Shutting off the live feed, she leaned back in her desk chair and rubbed her eyes. *What is wrong with me?* This type of erratic behavior usually happened to other people, not always-in-control Jessie, her legendary ability to stay unruffled the one good trait she inherited from her father. Despite usually remaining unflappable unless faced with the most stressful of situations—or her dad—she couldn't deny her feathers were rippling.

There was only one thing to do. Ignore the playbear from here on out. If she kept up her rude retorts and didn't give him an inch, he'd wander off and find someone else to torture—probably with his dick, making them scream in pleasure. A hiss escaped her, one of displeasure at the thought of Mason plying his wiles on someone else. *How can I be jealous?*

Jessie slammed her head down on the desk and groaned when her forehead hit the raised keys on her keyboard. *Am I so starved for attention or affection that I would find even a known heartbreaker's advances intriguing?* It irked to admit, even to herself, that she found him attractive.

Her phone rang. Glad for distraction, she grabbed it. "FUC technical department, Jessie speaking."

"Have you come to your senses yet?" The coldly voiced query by her father made her pinch the bridge of her nose in annoyance.

"Nothing wrong with my mind or senses, Dad. Working for a living is considered a respectable pastime, you know."

"Not when you're a princess," he retorted.

"Ah yes, how could I ever forget?" she drawled sarcastically. "Excuse me for wanting a life that doesn't involve ass kissing and fucking a stranger because you want an alliance."

"Watch your language, Jessica!" snapped her father.

"Sorry, Dad," she replied, because it was easier than listening to his diatribe if she told him to fuck off. Her fake apology didn't stop her from smiling that she'd managed to score one on the control freak.

"Whether you like it or not, as my daughter, you are a princess, and as such, you have duties to your family and your people. Your fiancé, whom you disparage, wouldn't be a stranger if you returned to the flock and resumed your duties."

"Not happening, Dad. I told you that before."

"You can't avoid this forever," her father warned. "Your fiancé is getting impatient. How long are you willing to force this charade? Is it war you want?"

"You're exaggerating." The Canadian swans were an easygoing flock for the most part. Her dad just wanted the alliance so he could take advantage of some of the great untouched lakes to the north of them. Apparently, it never occurred to him to just ask. Nope, he'd decided the best way to get a cheap vacation spot was to marry off his oldest daughter. And he wondered why he didn't get a present on Father's Day.

"Am I? How do you know how those crazy Canucks will take your obvious insult?"

"Whatever, Dad. This conversation is so over. Say hi to Aunt Matilda for me, would you?" She hung up before her father could utter another word. Every conversation recently sounded the same and she tired of it. When would her father realize that the life he'd planned for her just wouldn't happen, not if she had anything to say about it?

I don't care if I'm a bloody swan princess. I will marry who I want, when I want. Brave words, now if only she could get her dad to believe them—and not clip her flight feathers.

Chapter Three

Backup lab running at full capacity? Check.

Acquisition of new minions and the roundup of some old ones? Check.

Continuation of the research? Check.

New testing material? Check.

Regaining control of frozen financial assets? Pending.

Revenge against one bunny and bear? Argh!

Crumpling the list and flinging it across the room did little to alleviate the frustration. Since the disastrous loss of the main center of operations just over a month ago, it had taken time to get back up and moving in the direction of success again. The Moreau test facility did alleviate some of the issues regarding storage of specimens and available equipment; however valuable things, information mainly, and test subjects were still lost or in places too difficult to reach.

Then there was the money situation. Usually, a quick call to the man in charge of the purse strings at the defense department would have sufficed. Not any longer. Contacts in the human US military shied from overtures to resume their relationship. They rejected even the offering of free samples, fearful of the taint that might come from association.

But if they didn't want to play, then that was

their problem. The criminal element and rogue governments around the world had no such hesitancies and reached out with greedy hands for the chemical technology offered to them, for a price, of course.

Despite the bump in the road to success, and the hassles that still required solving, one thing remained in the forefront of the mind. Revenge, along with a need to acquire a precious sample of that damned werebunny's blood. With the minions back under control, the time to act was now before the agents at FUC discovered their misassumption.

Dead indeed. The report on the shifter news of a certain mastermind's demise was worth a good giggle, and made the plan to acquire one bunny by foul means so much easier.

They might have forgotten a little someone's name at the high school reunion—heck, most didn't even deign to acknowledge the diminutive presence unless it was to throw a casual "Ooops" when they trod into the unexpected shorty—but soon, everyone in the world would know the mastermind's name. Or at least the new and improved version.

Father and his squirelly ideas. A child's name should complement them, not subject them to ridicule. Yet another example of why the experiments were so important, as the ridicule would have never happened with a set of big teeth and the strength to rip limbs from tormentors.

And when I do finally cross that barrier from crossbred rodent to dangerous predator, I'll show them all.

Muah-ah-ah-choo. Damned allergies.

* * * *

A few weeks had passed since Mason dropped the bait bomb on Chase and his mate, a few weeks of utter boredom as he got assigned guard duty over his brother and Miranda. More like torture. Just how many times could one couple have sex in a day? If it weren't for their respective work schedules that spanned Monday to Friday, where they separated with long kisses and intimate gropes, Mason would have gone insane. As it was, the weekends just about killed him. Following them discreetly on nature walks so they could screw in the wilderness made him wish for winter. Watching them eye each other over a plate of pasta while they groped each other under the table made him lose all appetite. As for their stupid pet names for each? Honey bear and honey pie, gag him with a spoon. If he heard them say them one more time, he'd probably shoot himself.

And Jessie, that evil female whose presence haunted his dreams—and hardened his cock for a daily fisting in the shower—laughed when he complained.

"Why do I have to be in the apartment with them?" he moaned as she tapped away at her computer. Despite her numerous attempts to throw him out, he kept gravitating to her work area, drawn by the one woman who wouldn't drop her pants for him—even if he desperately wished she would. He'd not tapped a single pussy since he met the beauty with the tightly clamped thighs, and not because the offers were lacking. On the contrary, the women throwing themselves at him bordered on almost ridiculous and the more he gently turned them down, the harder they tried. They were coming at him with guns blazing, doing everything from wearing short skirts that left nothing to the imagination to gaping blouses, and even roaming hands.

Unfortunately, they didn't stir one iota of interest. Heck, his cock wouldn't even wake up, unless he accidentally thought of Jessie. One reminder of her dark eyes, her smirking lips, or her luscious ass and he became harder than a steel girder. He whacked off daily because of her, sometimes three times a day—huddled in a bathroom for privacy with the water running—and while his poor hand tired, no matter how many times he came grunting her name—her face in all its scowling glory so clear in his mind—it all ended up for naught as soon as he saw or thought of her again.

He knew the solution to his dilemma. A dip, or two or three, in the chocolate decadence that was Jessie; however, that didn't seem to be in the cards anytime soon. He swore she secretly delighted in shooting him down. He'd lost count at this point of how many times and ways she'd said no, yet, like a glutton for punishment, he kept going back. And he couldn't just blame his bearish curiosity. The man in him found her fascinating too.

"You need to be close by. The last time the mastermind decided to strike, cameras weren't enough," Jessie told him without even looking up from her keyboard. "Even though we've reinforced the firewall, and Frank, their bloody spy, is gone now, we're not taking chances this time that they'll slip someone past us."

"I get that part. But, you don't understand. They never stop."

"Stop what?" she mumbled absently.

"Having sex! What do you think?"

The fingers flying across her keyboard stumbled and halted. "Sure they do. I mean, they've got to eat, don't they?"

"They sometimes eat while doing it," Mason growled. "It's like a sickness with them." And annoying as hell since he wasn't getting any, and yet so desperately wanted some.

"I don't know what your problem is. I mean, you've spent, what, twenty years now keeping your neighbors up entertaining your lady friends? Shouldn't you be immune to women screaming?"

"First off, I am not that old." Although at twenty-eight and creeping, he'd certainly sown his fair share of oats. "Second, it's one thing to be involved in the creation of the screaming, another to have to listen to it. And we're not even going to discuss the grunting. It's my brother, after all, in there with her. It's gross."

"Nice to see you have some lines you won't cross," she replied, turning to give him a smirk that made her eyes crinkle with mirth.

"Why can't we get Viktor to do it for a few nights?" he grumbled. "I need a good fourteen hours uninterrupted rest. I'm a bear, you know, and we need our sleep."

"Viktor can't do it because Chase said he'd rip off the head of anyone else, which you well know. So stop pouting like a baby or I'll get you a pacifier and crazy glue it to your mouth."

"I know something else you can stick in my mouth." It slipped out before he could stop it.

"Yeah, my foot as it comes up through your ass. Now can it. Some of us are working here."

"You are so mean to me." And God, he loved it. Assertive, no nonsense, and so hot it made him hurt, Jessie embodied everything he wanted in a woman. Unfortunately, she seemed determined to resist him.

"Cry me a river. Go tell someone who cares." She said it, and yet, didn't enforce it, not like she had when he first started hanging out. The first week, she'd done everything she could to get him to leave. She peppered his lunch. Bruised his shins, kidney, and any other body part in reach. Stole his honey crueler. Called him fat—which sent him home to do pushups and sit-ups all night. She even tried to tell him she preferred women. That backfired when he told her that just made her hotter.

No matter how many times she acted like he was the biggest pain in her delectable, round ass, he could tell she secretly liked him, or at least tolerated his presence. He preferred to think like, though, because he'd not missed her occasional heated look when she thought no one watched. He even caught the sweet scent of her arousal on a few occasions. It gave him hope even when she treated him like he carried the plague, or a host of venereal diseases. Impossible. His shifter blood kept him clean.

"I am so underappreciated," he moaned dramatically.

Jessie snickered. "Gee, if only your numerous conquests could see you now, bitching and moaning like a little girl. What's wrong? Is your new schedule curtailing your sex life?"

"What sex life? I haven't seen a naked woman since I started working for FUC."

"Oh, poor baby. Are you suffering

withdrawal? I hear the sex emporium down the street is having a two for one sale on pocket pussies."

"Keep up the taunts and you can be part of the cure." Ooh, that changed the temperature in the room and added a musky scent he'd love to sniff from the source. Screw the mystery of a picnic basket, he'd take what Jessie hid in her pants any day.

As usual, though, she pretended dislike. "If you don't like the conversation, then go somewhere else to mope. Actually, I insist."

"But I like it here."

She swiveled in her chair and gave him the full effect of her brown-eyed gaze, more like glare, actually. It sent a shiver through him. "Why? Why do you keep coming back to my office? I don't like you. Hell, I'm not even nice to you. So why do you keep torturing us both?"

Because I'm a glutton for punishment. "Because, deep down, you don't hate me. You love me. Actually, you're dying to get your hands on my body and have your wicked way with me. And I just want you to know, I'm totally fine with that." He leered at her and waggled his brows.

She sighed. Loudly. But at least she no longer kicked him with her steel-toed boots. "You are such a freaking moron. I wouldn't have sex with you if all the dildos in the world turned into birds and flew away."

"You have a dildo?"

"No!" she yelled vehemently, but couldn't hide the telltale blush in her cheeks.

"You do, don't you?" he replied. "That is so freaking hot."

"Get out!"

"But I want to hear more about your dildo use. Like, do you use any lotion or just natural lube?"

He ducked as a stapler came flying his way. Then dodged as her keyboard followed. As he darted out the door, he couldn't help his parting, "Do you use Duracell or Energizer?"

The strangled yell made him grin from ear to ear.

Whistling, his hands shoved in his pockets to disguise the fact he sported a woody, he strolled back to his cubby hole of an office. Think room dividers, one scarred desk, and a pink laptop, all the FUC supply office had left when he went to get his office equipment.

Sitting in his chair, he spun, thoughts of Jessie filling his mind. He'd known her a few weeks now, and despite her brutal treatment of him, he totally wanted her. Getting her, though, proved quite the task. It didn't help that for every inch he struggled forward, she kicked him back a few feet. The woman went beyond ornery, but hot, oh so hot in her baggy cargo pants that hugged her hips and her logo t-shirts that clung to her full breasts. If only he could come up with an idea to get closer to her. Kidnapping her and holding her prisoner—naked in his bed—came to mind.

He'd tried the more conventional means first, but she refused all attempts to go out and she shot down all of his innuendos with suggested bodily harm. *What's a poor bear to do?*

Save her from danger? Kind of hard with her desk job.

Buy her lunch? The woman brought her own.

Slather her in honey and lick it off until she

changed her mind?

Mmm, honey. Hungry, he dug into a drawer and pulled out a caramel drop candy. He sucked on it as he pulled up the screen that showed the cameras monitoring his brother at work. Viktor watched over him, the wily crocodile hidden somewhere close by, but out of sight. His old unit buddy was a true mastermind when it came to subterfuge. As if sensing someone watched him, Chase, head bent over a stack of papers, raised a hand and shot him the middle finger.

Chuckling, Mason flipped his screen to see if the tracking devices embedded in their skin were still transmitting. The blue spot sat on the map in the right spot for Chase's office, while the bouncing red dot was smack dab in the FUC offices.

"What's up, doc?"

Miranda's chirpy greeting saw him shoot out of his chair and put the desk between them. Her toothy smile did nothing to reassure him. "Nothing. What's on your schedule for the day?"

A moue of distaste crossed her lips. "More paperwork. How am I supposed to be good bait if everyone keeps me cooped up all the time?"

"We just went for a walk last night in the park."

"Yeah, but Chase was with me. Who's going to be stupid enough to come after me with the scariest ol' grizzly in the world at my side?"

Mason couldn't help the snort. "Scariest? Really? Says the bunny with foot long fangs."

"Chase likes to protect me," she staunchly defended. "And I think it's cute. So don't you dare do or say anything to ruin it. Or else,"—she leaned in close and her tone turned menacing—"I'll unleash my bunny, and humiliate you in front of Jessie."

"Why would I care about being humiliated in front of Jessie? We're just coworkers."

Miranda blew him a raspberry. "Oh pl-l-l-ease," she drawled. "You look like some kind of moonstruck cow whenever she's around and I swear your tongue just about touches the ground. It's really quite pathetic, you know."

"Says the girl who bats her lashes at my brother every time he grunts."

"Yeah, but the difference between us is I'm getting some and you're not, grumpy." With a twitch of her nose and a sassy grin, Miranda hopped off again, leaving him to his misery.

Leaning back in his chair, he sank back into thoughts of Jessie. Or would have if his sixth sense, that never led him astray, would stop telling him something was wrong. He stood and began to walk toward the elevator, but found his feet veering away down the corridor instead that led to the lunch room and staff washrooms. His steps slowed as he approached the men's room, but his radar urged him to keep going.

A honk, a really pissed one, sounded, and he sprinted the rest of the way, his hand slapping the swinging door for the woman's washroom before he ran face first into it.

Locked? He didn't ponder the how or why; he just rammed a heavy shoulder into it, and when that barely budged the door, he reared back and gave it a boot.

With a crack, the door popped open and he charged through and went around a corner before stopping dead. A strange tableaux presented itself. Shreds of clothing littered the floor as a giant black swan with wings outspread and a red beak honked madly as it faced off against one ugly ass boar. Strangest of all, though, was Miranda stood behind the swan and actually looked…frightened.

"Call your bunny!" he yelled as he waved his arms to get the giant pig's attention.

"I can't."

Shit. Mason knew of only one reason why her body wouldn't transform. Chase would lose his mind. But lucky for her, Uncle Mason was here to save Miranda and whatever she carried in her belly. With a roar, he went grizzly. And totally badass, if he did say so himself.

Chapter Four

As timing went, his proved impeccable, and for the first time since she met him, Jessie found herself immensely glad to see Mason arrive. Actually, that wasn't entirely true. Her heart always skipped a beat at the sight of him, and she'd started bringing spare panties to work, but despite her body's enjoyment of his presence, her mind and heart refused to give in to the pleasure, or at least not without feeling guilt.

However, she allowed relief, and yes, happiness, to suffuse her when he arrived, a giant furry teddy to the rescue. Thank God she'd emptied her bladder before the whole mess started.

When she'd gone to pee, her short legs not touching the floor on the stupidly high toilets in the employee bathroom, she certainly never thought she'd have to come to Miranda's rescue, and from a most unlikely suspect.

Jessie had just wiped when she heard the happy whistle she knew so well. She just about called out a hello to Miranda when she heard Cecile from requisitions say, "Someone's been looking forward to getting their hands on you."

"What are you talking about?" was Miranda's reply, followed by, "Hey, what are you doing with that syringe? You know, you really shouldn't do drugs. They're bad for you."

"It's not for me, you stupid rabbit. I'm going to knock you out and bring you to the mastermind for my reward."

"Traitor!" Miranda spat.

"I prefer the term financially rewarded. Now be a good girl and let me stick you."

"Ha! Not likely. Prepare to meet my bunny."

Not worried—no one who knew Miranda would have been—Jessie waited, but the sound of ripping fabric never occurred. An evil chuckle sounded instead and Jessie used the noise to cover the rustle of her standing and pulling up her pants. She crept to the door and peered through the crack.

"Awww, is someone unable to shift? I knew if I bided my time it would happen and make my job easier."

"You won't get away with this," Miranda said, her defiant tone unwavering. "I might not be able to call my beast, but I can still kick your ass."

"In human shape, perhaps, but beat this, bitch."

Jessie flung open the bathroom stall as Cecile went from ugly and dumpy spinster to uglier, hairy pig with sharp tusks and beady red eyes.

"This isn't good," Miranda said, patting her hip for a firearm that wasn't there because of her desk duty.

Jessie didn't have a weapon either, or that many fighting skills for that matter, but it didn't stop her from shifting, her skin molting to reveal sleek black feathers, those on her wings tipped in white. She opened her red bill and honked. Waddling, she placed her body between the traitorous boar and her friend. Just because they didn't get their nails done together and she didn't give in to Miranda's suggestion of getting laid didn't mean she didn't like the woman. As a matter of fact, she did, and sometimes wished she could own some of her bubbly outlook on life.

Of course, bravery and the right thing didn't help her when faced with a wild-eyed, tusked and slavering beast. *This is not going to turn out well.* But on the bright side, she wouldn't have to get married. Prepared to meet her maker—and end up tenderized for swan pie—she honked again and flapped her wings, a swan's version of "Come and get me."

And then he appeared, bursting through the door like some action hero, distracting Cecile. As soon as Mason realized the dilemma, he turned furry, his towering grizzly facing off with the no-longer so frightening sow.

Shifting back to her human shape, albeit minus some clothes, Jessie whirled to check on Miranda, who clapped her hands in glee as a battle raged behind her that involved lots of crashing sounds.

"Are you okay?" Jessie asked.

"Me? I'm fine. Thanks for coming to the rescue, though."

"No problem." Jessie didn't quite know what else to say. Miranda did, though.

"Knock her on her ass, Mason!" Miranda hollered, not at all perturbed by the attack.

Crazy bunny. Jessie turned back to watch the action in time to see Mason take out Cecile with a swipe of his massive paw just as more agents came pouring into the room. Before Jessie could hide her naked state from the new crowd, something big and furry enveloped her.

"Hey!" she yelled, only to get a mouthful of fur for her exclamation. "What do you think you're doing?"

"He's protecting your modesty, I think," Miranda observed from beside her.

"He's also grabbing my ass," Jessie said through gritted teeth. She glared up at the big head and could have sworn the furry teddy smiled. He definitely squeezed one cheek.

Someone thrust clothes at her, but Jessie had to threaten to knee Mason in the balls to get him to reluctantly release her so she could back into a cubicle and throw on the emergency FUC track suit. With an office full of shape-shifters, one never knew when someone would need a spare set of clothes. When she emerged, Mason had just finished pulling up his pants, to the swooning delight of the office hens who clustered at the other end of the bathroom watching. For some reason, it ruffled her feathers. Not for long, though, as her eyes found themselves riveted by the wide expanse of chest before her. A hairy chest, she noted with interest, that covered him in a wiry pelt that led to a vee that disappeared in the waist band of his pants. She raised her eyes quick, but he caught her perusal and grinned.

"Did I dress too fast? I can strip if you'd like and start over."

"Oh like eew!" Miranda answered. Thank the avian gods, because Jessie almost said yes. "There's only one bear I like to see naked. Which reminds me, has anyone told—"

The roar that echoed down the hall and cleared the room answered the question of whether or not Chase knew about Miranda's close encounter.

Chase came tearing into the bathroom, his beast barely under control if the wild eyes were any indication. "Miranda! Are you okay?" he bellowed.

In a whirl of motion, Miranda leapt onto Chase, arms and legs folding around him in a tight vise. "I'm okay, honey bear. Jessie kept the bad girl at bay until Mason came to the rescue."

"Why didn't you take care of them yourself?" he asked, a crease forming between his brows.

A yank on her arm saw Jessie stumbling after Mason, who dragged her away from the about to get interesting scene.

"What are you doing? I want to see," she hissed.

"Unless you want to see them having sex, I suggest leaving now."

"But isn't she—"

"Going to tell him she's pregnant? Yes. And his reply is…" Mason paused as a hollered, "What?" made the air around them vibrate.

"I take it he's a little surprised?"

"Chase wanted to wait, but Miranda is Miranda." Another bellow preceded the cracking sound of someone's fist hitting something.

Jessie cast a startled glance behind her. "Should I be worried?"

"Nope, because whenever Miranda riles Chase up, usually on purpose, they end up naked and fucking within minutes."

A squeal of enjoyment made Jessie's mouth round into an O. "Um, shouldn't we put up, like, a sign or something warning people away?"

"Do you really think anyone is stupid enough

to come down here and gawk? You have met my brother, right?"

A wry grin tugged her lips. "I guess you have a point." It was then she noticed he held her hand even though they'd stopped to talk in the hall. She would have pulled away, but he laced his fingers tighter with hers.

"A swan, huh?" he said at her inquiring look. "I wouldn't have guessed."

And he'd apparently not cared enough to inquire given almost everyone in the office knew. "Why, because I'm not graceful and dainty?" she sniped.

"No, because I thought swans were white." He blanched as he said it and hurried to add, "Not that I'm racist or anything. Because I'm not. I love black. And white. And any color. Really, I do."

He looked so appalled, she laughed. "Your forehead needs a sign that says open mouth and insert one large foot here. Don't worry. It surprises most people. My mother was an Australian black swan. She migrated over here to marry my father, who is white, by the way."

"Have I mentioned I think you are really pretty? As a bird and a chick." He grinned, quite pleased at his play on words.

"And you're still not getting in my pants," she retorted, yanking her hand from his despite the fact she enjoyed the warmth of it wrapped around hers.

"Don't I at least deserve a kiss for saving your tail feathers?" He raised a hopeful brow. "Come on. I ruined my favorite pair of jeans saving your pretty neck."

About to tell him where to go shove his

expected reward, her mouth opened, and instead said, "One kiss." She almost looked behind her to see who'd put those words in her mouth. Surely she didn't want to kiss the bear who thought so highly of himself. Didn't want to feel those full lips of his against hers, sliding…

He didn't give her a chance to change her mind. He literally picked her up off the ground, his big hands spanning her waist and hoisting her face at a level with his.

"This is such a bad idea," she muttered as she drew close to the tempting lips that haunted her dreams—and all of her waking fantasies.

Then she couldn't think, just felt as his lips whispered across hers before pressing firmly, sending a jolt of awareness to shock her system. A gasp escaped her and she raised her hands to flatten them on his broad chest as he kissed her, a slow, sensual exploration of her mouth that left her breathless and aching for more.

It ended much too quickly with Mason setting her down suddenly and whirling. His broad body blocked her unsteady one from view.

"What are you dawdling for? I need to debrief you and Jessie," Kloe barked, unseen on the other side of Mason's body. "And when Miranda's done with whatever she's doing with Chase, she needs to give her report too."

Heat made Jessie's cheeks flush as she realized only Mason's quick thinking prevented her from getting caught making out at work, and with a known playbear of all people.

Well, at least now I know why the ladies love him. One kiss and I was just about ready to maul him myself.

As for him, apparently, it hadn't affected him the same way given he'd noted their boss's arrival. That cold dose of reality dispelled her arousal—or most of it. Squaring her shoulders, she moved around him to follow Kloe.

A hand shot out and grabbed her arm, halting her. "Jessie?"

The eyes regarding her held a bright glitter and seemed to say something, not that she could figure out what.

"You got your kiss. So consider yourself paid. Now, if you don't mind, we should get going before Kloe gets medieval on our asses."

He opened his mouth as if to speak, and stupid her, she actually wanted to hear him say, "Screw Kloe. Let's kiss again." Or even better, just do it. But instead, he clamped his lips tight and nodded.

Dejected, but not understanding why, she stomped up the hall, reminding herself of all the reasons why getting involved with a playbear was so wrong. But for some reason, the number one reason to give in kept trying to scream over her responsible list. And what was the number one reason to let Mason in her pants? Because it would feel so bloody good.

* * * *

Mason followed the delectable ass and had to shove his hands in his pockets lest he take a swipe at it, or even better, grab Jessie, throw her over his shoulder, and run for his cave, um, apartment. Ever since he'd caught a glimpse of her naked, a quick peek because an overwhelming possessive need came over him to hide the cocoa curves from everyone else, he'd wanted to taste her. The feel he'd copped of her ass just made him hungry for more. Letting her go so she could dress took willpower, but not as much as closing his eyes so he wouldn't embarrass her as she fled to a cubicle.

Thankfully, Miranda didn't peek at him while he dressed, or point and giggle at his woody. As if he could stop it from rising after holding his swan lady in his arms. Jessie luckily hid in a cubicle, not peeking according to the positioning of her feet while the office ladies tittered and gawked at his bare butt—which thankfully wasn't hairy like his dad's.

He didn't give a rat's ass about the reaction of the women behind him, not when he got the pleasure of seeing Jessie's eyes widen in appreciation when she emerged and saw his bare chest. It made a bear want to thump his ribs and strut around. Wait, wasn't that what gorillas did? Didn't matter. He still wanted to strut and gloat.

And then she agreed to a kiss, which surprised the hell out of him. He'd expected a kick in the shins along with a vehement no. What a nice surprise instead.

He went slow with her, letting his lips gently claim hers, inwardly rejoicing when she didn't shove him away. Talk about igniting his ardor, though. He could have kissed her all day. Probably would have, too, yet an instinct to protect made him hear the approaching steps. In a flash, he'd placed her behind him, the urge to keep his woman safe—*oh yes, my woman*—strong.

In retrospect, he should have just tossed her over his shoulder and run, anything to keep her lips soft and pliant under his instead of set in a mulish line that went well with her flashing dark eyes.

He blamed his bear's curious nature for wondering what her eyes would look like in the throes of passion. He blamed the man for plotting ways to ensure it happened. Both of his sides couldn't wait for his fantasy to become reality.

Still bare-chested, not daring to return for his shirt in the room holding his brother and a sighing bunny, he headed after Jessie and flopped on a chair beside her in Kloe's office.

Between him and Jessie, they got Kloe up to speed, the frown between her brows deepening with each word. At the end, his boss leaned back in her chair and sighed. "This isn't good. We never even suspected Cecile was a spy and, trust me, we were thorough after the Frank fiasco."

Frank used to be a trusted agent in the FUC office until it was discovered he leaked secrets for money. He died after trying to kidnap Miranda, and a witch hunt ensued in the FUC offices across the country. But they never did find any more spies, even if Mason suspected they existed.

"What are we going to do to protect them?" Jessie asked. "With Miranda pregnant and unable to shift, she can only defend herself with her bare hands."

"She's far from defenseless," Kloe remarked dryly. "That girl could shoot a short hair off a charging bull if she needed to. And I think her grizzly mate would have a problem with someone messing with his bunny. But I agree, with the change in her status, we can no longer use her as bait."

"Nor can we trust FUC to protect her," Mason added.

"Hey!" Jessie threw him an indignant look.

"I'm not talking about anyone in this room, but all it takes is one more Cecile, someone under our radar, for things to go to hell."

Kloe inclined her head. "So what's your suggestion then?"

"They need to go underground. I'd recommend putting them under the protection of a special ops member. And lucky you, we have one handy. Viktor knows what to do. He can assemble a team of shifters he trusts to aid him."

"I'm surprised you wouldn't offer to take them yourself."

Mason smiled, not his usual jovial grin, but the toothy one of a predator who'd suddenly discovered something tasty to eat. "And miss the fun hunting the mastermind down and ripping him a new one? No, I'll stay right here glued to Miss Tech Geek's butt until she deciphers some more of the mumbo jumbo on those hard drives we recovered. I want to be here when we find out where the bastard is holed up."

"I don't need you breathing down my neck," Jessie retorted.

"I'll breathe down whatever body part I want if I think it will get us answers," he snapped. "And you'll be glad of the help, or did it escape your notice that had I not arrived, we'd be having roasted swan for dinner?"

"Cannibal."

"Try realist."

"Interesting as this conversation is, we seem to have veered off topic. Jessie, the bear is right. We really need that information more than ever, so as of now, I'm releasing you from your regular duties to concentrate solely on the drives we recovered. We'll call in another techie from another office to cover your regular duties. Mason, I'll want you to re-run background checks on all the office agents. I can't understand how anyone could work for the sicko, but I guess money speaks louder sometimes than integrity."

"We'll catch him," Mason quietly promised. Catch the sick little fucker and make him pay.

Dismissed, Mason followed Jessie back to her office. She flopped in her chair and immediately began typing.

A crease between his brow, Mason spun her chair so she faced him. "Don't you think we should talk?"

She wouldn't meet his gaze, staring instead at his feet. "About? Kloe gave us our orders. I'll let you know when I find something."

Stubborn chick. His hands itched to shake her. "I meant about the kiss."

She raised her head and blinked. "What about the kiss?" She tried to sound nonchalant, but she seemed to forget his keen hearing, which caught her increased heart rate.

"There's something between us." He stated it boldly and waited for her reply. And yes, dammit, a hopeful part of him wanted her to acknowledge it.

"Yeah, mutual dislike." She blatantly lied, but couldn't help licking her lips, her eyes straying to peek at his mouth.

She could pretend all she wanted. His gut knew better. "It's not dislike."

"Speak for yourself."

"Are you really going to deny the spark between us?" *Oh yes, deny it, baby, so I can prove you wrong.*

"Yup. What you felt was me being grateful that you saved my feathers from getting plucked. Nothing more."

"Really?" He didn't bother hiding the dangerous glint that entered his eyes at her implied challenge. "Then you won't have a problem proving it."

"I—um, that is—"

He crouched down so their faces were level. "I think," he said, tilting her chin up when she would have avoided his gaze, "that you liked that kiss. Actually, more than liked it, and I think it scares you."

"You don't frighten me."

"Then kiss me again. If there's nothing there like you claim, then no harm, and I'll leave you alone."

"We really shouldn't." She whispered the words, but couldn't tear her gaze from his mouth.

"Then how will you prove me wrong?"

Before she could answer, a rustle at the door had Mason standing and whirling to see a guy almost his height, thickly muscled and sporting a crown of downy platinum hair. The stranger's cold blue eyes only briefly took in Mason's presence before shifting to Jessie.

"Jessica. I heard about your mishap and as I was in town, thought I would come by and see if you were okay." The guy spoke stiffly, and Mason wondered who the uptight dick was. *And what does he want with my Jessie?*

"Eric, you really shouldn't have bothered." Jessie's frosty tone didn't deter the blond giant, also some kind of bird by the whiff of him, from approaching Jessie and dropping to his knees in the position Mason just left.

"Of course I did. Actually, I was going to call you anyway. I'm in town on business for the week and I was hoping we could get together for dinner."

"No."

Mason couldn't help a triumphant grin as she shot the stranger down. "You heard the lady. Now say goodbye. We have work to do." Work that involved getting her to admit she wanted him.

The icy blue gaze met his for a brief moment, and Eric's jaw tightened. "This is none of your concern." Then the guy dismissed him and turned back to face Jessie. "I realize the situation is distasteful, but this is about more than you and me. Can't we at least make an attempt?"

The conversation, for some reason, struck a discordant chord and Mason couldn't help asking, "Jessie, who is this clown?"

Sighing, Jessie's gaze met his, her expression a blank mask. "Mason, meet Eric, my fiancé."

The room might have reeled, that or the earth tilted on its axis because something shot his equilibrium to hell. "I didn't know you were engaged," he managed to say instead of what he really wanted to do, which involved going on a furry rampage.

The blond stood and held out a hand, a smirk on his lips. "Eric Peters. I'm from the Canadian flock, here on business and, hopefully, pleasure."

Mason couldn't avoid shaking the other man's

hand, who, annoyingly enough, possessed a firm grip despite his pansy-looking hair and suit.

"Well, I guess I should let you and your fiancé have some alone time," Mason said, pasting a fake smile on his face.

"Mason." Jessie appeared troubled, but she did nothing to stop him when he left. A good thing too, because he might have just given in to his need to grab her and run far, far away and make love to her until she forgot the uptight dick who already had a claim to her.

At least her engagement explained why she kept shooting him down, although why she wouldn't have thrown that in his face at the first opportunity he didn't understand. And why had she agreed to kiss him? He'd not taken Jessie for the type of woman to cheat on a lover. Then again, she appeared to treat Eric with even more disdain than she did Mason. Why would she have agreed to marry someone she seemed to barely tolerate?

And why did he want to know?

He should have thanked his lucky stars that he'd found a really good reason to forget Jessie. To stay away from her barbs and sharp tongue. Away from her irresistible scent and… Dammit, engaged to get married or not, it seemed he still wanted her.

Time to get drunk. Right after he made sure Viktor secreted Miranda and his brother away. Then, he was going on a date with a big bottle of tequila. Maybe two.

Chapter Five

Damn FUC and their witness protection program. They'd hidden the bunny well, her and her ornery mate. They'd also made her entire family disappear, foiling the plot to acquire a sample of blood. With the spy discovered and jailed in the deepest, darkest pit FUC could find, the possibility of finding out where they'd stashed the bunny and her family was a great big zero. It made a person want to stomp their feet and gnash their teeth.

But tantrums would accomplish nothing. The time had come to move on from the werebunny and concentrate on others. Sometimes the path to success needed to snake sinuously around its prey, binding the coils of a trap tighter and tighter until escape became impossible. Hence, plan B, already put into motion and which would provide a new level of entertainment. Sure, the current target was more of a challenge, but taking the easy route smacked of cowardice. It would be better to practice boldness and daring now so that when size and teeth were achieved, acts of temerity would become second nature. Besides, the current target was the next best thing to Miranda and her bear.

The door to the sanctum burst open. "The package has been delivered," said the hyena with a barely restrained giggle, a loyal henchman who'd returned to the fold more eager than ever to serve.

"Excellent." Drumming fingers on the desktop, a bubble of glee—the evil, mastermindish kind—burst free. *Muah-hihihi. Muah-hihihi.*

* * * *

A week had passed since the kiss—or as Jessie remembered with disgust, seven long days since Mason found out about her fiancé and dropped her like a hot potato. Needless to say, her week sucked and she owed everything to the fact one big, annoying bear stopped dropping in to drive her nuts. She should have rejoiced he finally got the hint. Instead, she ended up morose and eating chips like they were going out of style.

To make matter worse, she kept having to turn down polite requests to dinner from her equally reluctant fiancé. Poor guy. He was just as much a victim of birth as she was, but unlike her, he didn't seem inclined to fight it as hard. What a shame she couldn't find a single spark of interest in the blond swan, anything to make her life easier. To add insult to an already annoying situation, she also had to dodge the angry diatribes of her father who seemed to have issues with her decision to ignore the visiting Canadian prince. The conversation tended to devolve into name calling and threats, usually after her dad yelled, "I am your father. You will do as you're told." To which she usually replied, "Screw you and the tail wind you flew in on." Boy, did things get ugly after that. But at least her father gave her an outlet to vent, not that it helped much.

All in all, she'd never been more miserable, so when Kloe buzzed her to say the FUC receptionist had received a suspicious package, Jessie had scurried as quick as her short legs could to the reception area, tool box in hand. A trip to the emergency room sounded a lot more fun than her current plan of going home to mope and stuff her face with yet more chips her ass didn't need.

As a precaution, and according to the safety manual some stiffs in penguin suits created, the FUC staff on duty were sent home early just in case the innocuous container contained something nefarious. *I should be so lucky*. The employees, about two dozen or so, filed out quickly, no one wanting to mess with a chance to leave early while still getting paid. Once the place got quiet, she got to work.

Jessie and Kloe peered from opposite sides at the package with way more interest than it deserved. A plain brown box, taped with clear packing tape on all the seams, it bore a white label with the FUC address written in block letters and no return address.

"What do you think is in it?" Kloe whispered.

"Why are you whispering?" Jessie asked in a low hush herself.

"What if there's a pressure switch inside, you know, a noise activated one?"

Jessie snorted, loudly. "You did see the delivery guy who brought it, right? He was almost bloody juggling it while singing Rihanna off key. Nope, if it's a bomb, something else is the trigger." Pulling down her goggles over her eyes, she leaned in to peer at the package, her lenses distorting the item before her. Varying colors and shading appeared based on the density and warmth of the item and its contents. She saw nothing that rang any alarm bells. She ran a radiation wand over the mysterious box next, but not even a blip registered. A fingerprint scan came up blank as well.

Cocking her head, Jessie shoved her infrared goggles up on her forehead, pushing her bangs up in a tuft on top of her head. She pursed her lips as she tried to think of another exterior test to run before she slit open the tape.

"What are we looking at?"

Mason's exaggerated whisper from right behind her ear made her scream and jump, her arms flailing in panic and catching the corner of the package. They all turned to watch as if in slow motion—their expressions more than likely comical in their horrified sameness—as the innocuous box fell to the ground on its side.

Jessie blinked, her body tense as it waited for a reaction. Nothing happened. She whirled and pummeled a rock hard chest. "You idiot! What if that had been a bomb?"

"But it smells like cookies," he said, not even flinching from her attack.

Stupid bear. "What do you mean it smells like cookies? I don't smell anything." Jessie stopped hitting him so she could bend down and pick up the package. She stuck her nose right up to it. Inhaling deep, she smelled nothing unless cardboard counted.

"Trust me when I say it smells like cookies. Heck, I won the championship for picnic basket sniffing and guessing three years in a row. So are you really going to argue with me about this when you know for a fact birds don't have the greatest sense of smell?"

A glower was his reply.

"As a connoisseur of confectionary and other baked goods, I can say that these are triple chocolate…" Mason sniffed again. "With raisins and oatmeal."

"Poisoned ones, I bet."

He blew his lips in a loud raspberry. "Okay, oh suspicious one. Shall we dissect one and find out?"

"Why don't you do that while I go and question the delivery boy a little further?" Kloe said before sneaking off as they stood staring at each other.

Jessie couldn't help drinking in the sight of him. He'd made himself scarce since the fiasco and seeing him again brought back in a rush all the reasons why he haunted her mind. Looking as yummy as ever, his t-shirt hugged his chest and tucked into even snugger jeans. God, she just wanted to jump on him and tear the clothes from his body and…

Do really dirty things.

Bad swan. She gave herself a mental shake and tried to make sure she kept an aloof expression on her face, or at least something that didn't scream, "Take me! Take me now!"

His lips quirked, though, as if he'd guessed her thoughts anyway. "You heard the boss. Let's go test these cookies." He swept an arm out, letting her lead with the package. Talk about self-conscious. She wondered if he checked out her butt. Probably not given she wore a long sweater today over her many pocketed khakis. But in case he did, a little extra wiggle never hurt.

Was it foolish to hope for a playful slap on her derriere then to feel disappointed when it didn't come?

She plopped the package on her desk with more force than necessary and dropped into her chair. Staring at the package for a moment, she mentally went over any more tests she could run before opening it. A groan distracted her, a sensual rumble that sent shivers skating down her spine.

What the hell? Swiveling on her seat, she blinked at what she saw. Mason, his eyes partially shuttered, grunted again as he rubbed his big body back and forth across the edge of the door frame. It was fascinating. Odd too, and yet sensual.

"What are you doing?"

"Scratching."

She watched him vigorously swaying from side to side, even up and down, his back pressed hard against the corner. He made sounds of enjoyment as he did, and looked so much like a bear in that moment, even wearing his human skin, her lips twitched. "You are a freak," she exclaimed, shaking her head at his strange behavior.

"But I'm itchy. If it bothers you so much, you could offer to scratch it for me." He winked and put his hands to the hem of his shirt, pulling it up a few inches to display taut abs.

She swallowed as her mind so easily conjured an image of him stripping his shirt the rest of the way and kneeling so she could touch the broad expanse of his back. God, the bear knew how to tempt her. "Get a back scratcher," she snapped instead before whirling back to the package.

"Spoilsport," he muttered. Mason parked himself on the corner of her desk while she pulled out a pocket knife. She aimed it at the package.

"Aren't you going to check it for prints?" he

asked.

"We already did before you arrived. It's clean."

She sliced through the tape on one seam, parting it neatly on all sides. Then, she took a deep breath and was about to pull open the top when Mason snatched it from her desk and turned with it.

"Hey, what are you doing?"

"I'm opening it just in case I'm wrong and it is dangerous. I figure my face is more expendable." He turned back and held out the box with a flourish.

"You idiot. What if you were wrong about the contents?"

He shrugged. "Chicks dig scars. But enough about my bravery and self-sacrifice. You can thank me later if you want, naked." He waggled a hopeful brow. She growled, more because her body reacted instantly to his suggestion. "Can't fault a bear for trying. Since I'm not getting rewarded for my act of courage, let's see what's inside."

"You are such an idiot." But still, his unexpected chivalry did please her—and his hope they'd get naked together made her hotter than a shot of brandy on a cold winter's night.

He set the box on her desk and she peered in to see a Ziplock bag filled with cookies. "Why would someone send us cookies anonymously?" she mused.

"Because they like us and want to say thank you for doing a great job?"

"Or they want to poison us."

"Always so negative," he chided.

"I prefer to call it cautious," she stated as she lifted the bag out and held it up to peruse under a fluorescent lamp. Honestly, she didn't know what she looked for. She wasn't a chemist, or even a baker, although she and Betty Crocker got along just fine. Setting the cookies down, she bent over to open her bottom drawer and pull out a manila envelope.

"What are you doing?" Mason asked.

"Sending it to people who can actually test these things, of course. I do electronics and stuff, not baked goods."

"But that will take too long."

"You have another plan?" she asked as she browsed her list of contacts for the address of their lab.

"Yup." A plastic rustle was all the warning she got. She turned and gaped in horrified astonishment as she saw Mason pop a cookie into his mouth.

"Are you insane?" She shouted the words, panic clawing her as he chewed, a thoughtful expression on his face.

"Mmm. Not that I know of. So I was right— chocolate, raisins, oatmeal, oh, and a hint of cinnamon. They're actually pretty good." He popped another in his mouth.

"Mason." She almost moaned his name as he ate another possibly poisoned treat. "Are you suicidal? Is that it?"

"Oh live a little, Jessie. Not everything is a trap."

"Says the man who might have less than a minute to live."

His eyes met hers, a smoldering intensity entering them. "Well, if I'm about to croak, then shouldn't you give a dying man one last kiss?"

"This is not the time for you to hit on me."

But she couldn't help staring up at his mouth, hunger invading her at the thought of tasting his lips again.

He dropped to his knees before her, which brought him just below the level of her face, and peered at her. "I think this is the perfect time. As a matter of fact, I think I'm feeling faint. Quick, kiss me, Jessie. Give a dying bear something to live for." He even added a choking sound at the end of his plea.

She would have said no. Most definitely. But he leaned in close before she could and claimed her mouth, actually more than claimed; he possessed it. Utterly. Thoroughly. Decadently. *Oh, heavenly.*

His lips clung to hers, moving in ways she never imagined possible, tugging at her own, massaging her sensitive flesh. A gasp of shock escaped her at the need that flooded her with his touch, and he took full advantage. Slipping his tongue into her mouth, the sweetness of the chocolate cookie lingering, he tasted her and let his tongue dance along hers.

She didn't remember sliding from her chair, or how she came to be sitting in his lap, her legs straddling him as his hands cupped her buttocks. Not that she cared because she kissed him back with a fierceness she never expected. A need she'd never experienced. With each sensual caress, each erotic lick, every aching touch, she forgot everything but her pleasure, a pleasure only Mason could give her.

Her fingers tangled in his hair, pulling him close. Heat invaded her limbs, setting her whole body tingling and creating an ache in her sex. Her cleft moistened in expectation. How could it not with the hard bulge rubbing against her, promising delight? Showing such ardent desire?

He pulled away, and she let out a mewl of displeasure before opening lids heavy with passion.

"We have to stop," he groaned as his hands massaged her buttocks.

"What?" His comment made no sense, not when she could feel his need still pressing against her core. She didn't want to stop, not when her whole body felt like it would explode if she didn't finish what they'd started. For the first time since she'd discovered sex—in the back seat of a car in a thirty second tussle that left her mouth agape in astonishment over the boredom of the act—she got the impression she'd discover why so many people threw caution and common sense to the wind for a bout of pleasure. Maybe she would experience an orgasm without the use of her own fingers, or dildo. Or would if he'd get back to kissing and groping her.

"I can't believe I'm saying this, but we can't do this. It wouldn't be right. You're engaged," he reminded her.

Oh, talk about a cold water shower of reality. With a gasp, more of horror this time, she clambered off his lap and slapped a hand to her mouth. Her lips still tingled from his touch and she could still taste him on her tongue. God help her, she wanted more.

"Get out." She said it softly, a tremble running through her body at the smoldering look in his eyes that said he also wanted her just as much. But if he did, then why stop?

"Jessie." He held out a hand. "We need to talk about this. About us."

"There is no 'us.' There can never be an 'us.'" She moved away from him and the temptation he evoked. She shook her head. "You're right. We can't do this."

"Because you're engaged to another." He almost spat his claim as if the very words tasted foul in his mouth.

Jealousy? Surely not. She squashed the tendril of pleasure at the thought. "We can't do this, but not because of Eric. Even if I weren't engaged to him, you and me, it can't happen. For one thing, I don't do one night stands."

"Who says it's for one night? You do things to me, Jessie. Make me feel shit I've never felt before."

"Nice line, use it often?" She snarled the word at him, suddenly all too mindful of his reputation.

"Never. What I feel for you is new. Special."

"I don't believe you."

"I don't lie. You're special, Jessie."

"Don't do this." She shook her head wildly, trying to deny his surely false claim.

"Do what? Tell you I've come to care for you? Tell you that I can't stop thinking of you. Tell me you don't feel the same thing. That you don't think of me when you're alone. Come on, I dare you."

How did he know? Were her reluctant feelings for him so noticeable? "I'll admit you get my motor running, but I'm not spreading my legs for sixty seconds of grunting just because you make me hot."

"First off, when we make love, it's going to take more than a minute, and you'll be screaming my name long before I get to come. That's a promise."

"So you'd give me an orgasm. Whoopee. I can do that myself, and guess what? I don't have to worry about getting dumped the next day."

Annoyance began to overcome the look of

passion on his face. "Dammit, what part of I want you for more than sex do you not grasp? Give me a chance. Is that so hard?"

"Um, I'm still engaged, or had you forgotten?"

"Yeah, I had forgotten because any idiot can see you don't love him. What I don't get is if you don't give a shit about your fiancé, why not dump him?"

Why indeed. "It's complicated."

"So explain it."

"I'm a swan." A feeble excuse that made him arch a brow.

"No shit. And I'm a bear. There's no law against our kind getting together."

She chewed her bottom lip. How much should she tell him? Only Kloe knew about her actual rank in the flock. "I'm not just a swan. I'm a swan princess."

He blinked. Looked her up and down, then blinked again before he broke out into loud laughter.

"What's so funny?" she asked, planting her hands on her hips.

"Oh come on. A swan princess? Couldn't you have come up with a better excuse? Maybe something a little more believable?"

"But it's true. My dad is the swan king, which makes me a princess, and as such, I'm expected to make a marriage of convenience with another of my kind, one that will strengthen our flock."

His laughter broke off. "Seriously? So, what, this Eric clown is some kind of political dude and your dad arranged the wedding?"

"Exactly."

"Bullshit."

"Excuse me?"

"You heard me. I think you're full of it. I've known you what now, a month? There is no way you'd ever marry some freakn' noob you don't like just because your daddy says so, swan princess or not."

Okay, he did kind of know her. But still... "I resent that. I take my family and obligations very seriously."

"I'm sure you do, but I highly doubt you'd let anyone tell you who to fuck and have babies with."

Gee, he'd almost quoted word for word her last yelled statement to her dad. "I don't think who I agree to screw or why is any of your business," she replied stiffly.

"Oh it is, baby. Because you like me. And I like you. It's only a matter of time now before we end up in bed together."

Damn, not exactly the most romantic of speeches, but it still made her heart beat faster, which, in turn, annoyed her. "Cocky bastard, aren't you? Not likely."

"Liar." He stepped closer to her and she moved back only to hit her desk.

"What are you doing?"

"I am going to prove you can't resist me."

"I'm engaged."

"It's an arranged one so I have decided it doesn't count."

Her mouth gaped open. "What do you mean you've decided it doesn't count? I've got the ring at home to prove it does."

"Take me home and show me then." He

arched a brow in challenge and, dammit, she almost took him up on it. Already she could picture herself showing it to him and him throwing it out of a window before he tossed her onto a bed and had his wicked way with her. Oh God, did she want him to have his wicked way with her.

How could she stop this? How could she make him leave? There had to be something she could do or say to make him go away. To remove the temptation. "You're just going to make me say it, aren't you?"

"Say what?" he murmured, pushing his body into hers, his hard frame flush against her voluptuous one.

"You're not good enough for me." She fought not to cringe as she said it.

His whole body went rigid. "Excuse me?"

"You heard me. I'm royalty and you're just some bear. I mean, really think of it. You're a muscle bound, glorified soldier, and a manwhore to boot. You can't seriously think you're good enough for me." The filthy words poured from her mouth and made her stomach roil. They went against everything she believed in, but were familiar because she'd heard variations of it all of her life from her father, a true interspecies and class snob.

"You've eschewed the life a royal, obviously, or you wouldn't be here."

"Maybe, but it doesn't change the fact I'm black and you're white. Mixed couples don't do well in society."

"Un-fucking-believable. I can't believe you just said that." He growled the words.

She inhaled deep before meeting his angry

gaze. It took everything she had not to flinch. "Yeah, well, I tried to tell you to go away nicely, but I guess you're just too dumb to understand, white boy. Not your fault. I mean, you are from peasant stock after all." Oh, there was surely a special place in hell reserved for her now. But, with that vile insult, she got the result she wanted. She couldn't have made him more pissed if she'd kicked him in the balls. He spun on his heel and left.

A part of her couldn't believe it worked even as she watched him strut off, his back ramrod stiff and angrier than she'd ever seen him or thought him capable. *I managed to make the second happiest person I've ever met—because no one beats Miranda—miserable.* She deserved a trophy for bitch of the year. But at least it worked.

Sinking into her chair, a numbness invaded her limbs. She'd done the right thing—*I think*—or had she? Hard to tell with the tears clogging her throat and brimming in her eyes. Without even thinking twice about it, she grabbed a cookie and ate it, the flavor making the tears roll in a steady stream as they reminded her of the sweetness of Mason's kiss. She ate them all save one, sanity returning at the last possible moment.

Packaging the one cookie up and sealing it in the envelope was done in a fuzzy haze. That disembodied feeling followed her as she walked home, her steps wavering as her vision blurred.

What the hell? Even misery couldn't account for the lethargy seeping into her limbs.

Too late it occurred to her that she'd been right about the damned cookies. Of course, gloating would have to wait if the skulking figures that emerged from the alley were any indication.

She spun to run back to the safety of the FUC offices, but her feet tangled, and she pitched head first toward the pavement. Her last thought before darkness hit? *Murphy's gotten me back for being so mean to the bear.*

Chapter Six

Mason hit the men's room door, his shove ramming the swinging portal into the wall, his rage barely under control.

How could she feed me that line of shit about me not being good enough for her?

Because he recognized bullshit when he heard it. Even she hadn't been able to completely stem her distaste at the crap she fed him. Nor could she hide her desperation to make him leave.

It hurt him. Him! The man who'd bedded more women than probably all his buddies combined. Him, who'd never gotten rejected before. And now, when he found himself completely and utterly intrigued—and hornier than he'd ever imagined—the one woman he truly wanted above all others didn't want him back.

Worse, he didn't understand why.

She freely admitted Eric—her fiancé whose face needed to meet his fist—was nothing but something her dad wanted. He knew, with a certainty his brother Chase would have scoffed at, that she didn't give a rat's ass about her royalty status or the quality of his blood or her ridiculous assertion that because of their color they couldn't be a couple. So what truly sent her running?

Manwhore.

The word came into his mind from nowhere, haunting and taunting him with his past exploits. In that moment, a frightening clarity hit him. She feared him because she honestly thought he wanted her as just another notch on his bedpost. But he'd told her otherwise. Told her he'd come to care for her.

And she'd freaked right out. Could the answer be as simple as trust? If yes, how could he make her see she meant something to him? That he truly wanted her for more than a quick screw?

Mason paced the bathroom in agitation, and stumbled as his feet dragged. *What the fuck?*

Dizzy, he held out a hand to the wall and steadied himself. He shook his head and fought back against the languor that thought to creep through his limbs. *Shit, Jessie was right.*

The cookies were drugged, but with what and for what purpose? Was the mastermind looking for new specimens to experiment on? Were they even now lying in wait for the idiot who'd fallen into their trap to come stumbling out of the building incapacitated and an easy victim?

Like hell. He'd only eaten two, and he'd always enjoyed a great recuperative ability, one honed during his years in the special ops as they trained their soldiers to resist a bevy of chemical attacks. Mason stuck his head under the cold water tap and alternated sucking back mouthfuls and letting it run over his face. The briskness of the chilly liquid revived him and he flung his head back to let out a satisfied burp.

That felt better; however, a nagging thought struck him as clarity returned. What if someone else ate some of the drugged cookies? Not likely given

Jessie didn't trust them and had probably already packaged them for mailing to the lab, but just in case...

Mason strode back through the empty FUC halls to Jessie's work area. He found the package on her desk, the label written in sloppy loops and scrawls so unlike her usual tidy script. Lifting the bubble wrap envelope, Mason shook and weighed it. Horror made him drop the too-light package that held only one tantalizing perfume on its surface. *She ate some!*

Mason sprinted from the office and bypassed the elevator in favor of leaping down the stairs, vaulting his weight over the railing and hopping from landing to landing with a thump. He hit the main lobby and ran, sprinting through the glass doors into the swiftly encroaching night.

He scanned the street, but saw no sign of Jessie. Taking a deep breath, he let his nose filter the myriad scents. He almost dropped to his knees in thanks when he got a whiff of a familiar citrusy perfume. He took off jogging, anxiety making his heart tight while adrenaline made his legs pump like pistons.

And still, he almost arrived too late. He saw Jessie, wearing her familiar army jacket and bright red hat, fall to the ground right at the feet of a pair of hulking figures.

Letting out a roar not often heard outside the forest, Mason charged the men who snagged his Jessie and tossed her into a waiting cargo van. The thugs leapt into the van, but before it could pull away, Mason leapt onto the hood, crumpling it as he slammed a fist into the windshield. The glass cracked. Another thump of his fist and it honeycombed into pieces that fell inside the cab of the vehicle. Of course, that made the task for the guy pointing the gun at his forehead much easier.

"Move and I'll blow your brains out," the pock-faced stranger said, a wild light in his eyes daring him to.

Great, he'd run into a fucking hyena. Crazy fucking bastards. But Mason wasn't afraid for himself. He'd faced worse odds before. Even had the scars to prove it. He smiled. "You messed with the wrong fucking bear." He no sooner said it when he sprang lightning quick up onto the top of the truck, not stopping when he hit, but rolling the length of it to the back while listening and counting the number of rounds the hyena fired.

One, two, three…

A full-sized, 9mm Glock held up to seventeen rounds. When the pockmarked driver stopped firing after six, Mason jumped up from where he knelt at the back and charged toward the front. Instead of firing again, the fucker started the engine. Mason flattened himself, scrambling for hand holds as the truck screamed away from the curb. His legs still went swinging as his fingers strained to hold on. Then he went flying as the driver slammed the brakes. Tucking and rolling, Mason landed and popped up, finally pulling his own revolver free from his ankle holster in one fluid motion. Tires spun as the van made to leave.

Pop. Pop. Mason flattened the two front tires, and strode back toward the idling vehicle, firing again into the engine, making it sputter and die.

Bodies poured out of the van and, suddenly,

the night was rife with whizzing bullets. One lodged in his upper forearm, not that it mattered. Special ops always trained them to fire equally well with either hand. Flipping his weapon to the other hand, he zig-zagged his course while firing. He winged one scumbag in the wrist and with a scream of pain, one gun left the fight. A bullet tore into his thigh, making him grunt, but he ignored the pain, more thankful the morons didn't know how to shoot a moving target. Weaving erratically toward them, he fired off a few quick shots and heard another yelp, followed by running feet as the hyena and the last two henchmen standing took off.

Mason, now level with the van, hesitated, torn between a desire to hunt the fuckers down and his need to check on Jessie. His fear for her saw him clambering into the van. He found her slumped on the floor in the back, slack jawed and snoring. Lifting her into his arms, he checked her visually for injury, but saw nothing other than a blooming bruise on her forehead.

The strident wail of sirens filled the night, their sound increasing as they approached. Leaping from the van, wincing at the pain in his thigh when he did so, he walked about twenty feet away first before turning and firing into the gas tank. The spark from his shot ignited it, and he turned quickly to run, hunching over his precious burden in case stray debris should come flying as the vehicle behind him caught fire.

Under more controlled circumstances, he would have called FUC and had them tow it in along with the two bodies lying alongside it, but with human authorities on their way, he needed to act quickly to hide the evidence. Shootouts occurred in the city all the time, however, the one thing no shifter ever wanted was for the humans to get their hands on their blood.

As it was, their local police scrubber, a mole on the force, would probably have to make certain pieces of evidence disappear lest anything rouse suspicions. Shifting Jessie in his arms, Mason went a few blocks, keeping close to buildings and shadows, avoiding the curious glance of strangers. Apathy was strong in the city, which was probably the only reason he got away with carrying his precious burden.

Eventually, he made it back to the FUC building, and his car in the underground parking. More cautious now, he silently apologized to Jessie as he slung her limp form over his shoulder so he could pull out his gun again and keep it in front of him as he crept to his vehicle. Nothing jumped out, and with a sigh of relief, he gently placed her in the back seat of his Dodge Challenger. He winced as he sank into his seat. Not because of the pain of his wounds, but because of the blood stains he'd surely leave on the custom leather seats.

Driving to his home, a condo on the top floor of a waterfront development that had gotten more use in the last month than the last few years combined, he thanked his stars for the elevator that, once in motion, didn't stop for anyone else until it discharged its current occupant. A high-tech feature for those like himself who preferred privacy even when so close to home.

Placing Jessie on his bed gave him a perverse pleasure even though he knew she'd probably lose her mind and hurt him. But still, that didn't stop him from removing her hat and coat, as well as her boots. He covered her with a comforter before heading back out to his living room to report in.

He needed to hold his cellphone away from his ear as Kloe understandably freaked, ranting about their irresponsibility in eating the damned cookies in the first place. He could only quietly agree, chagrined that his careless disregard for his own safety put Jessie in danger. However, despite his stupidity, something good did come out of the whole ordeal. Kloe ordered him to guard Jessie, day and night, in case the drugging attempt was a targeted rather than random one.

What a chore. Protect his swan princess. Glue himself to her body to keep her from harm. God, he loved his job sometimes. He gladly agreed to his new job description and hung up with his boss.

Debriefing out of the way, he finally gathered and lay out the medical supplies on the bathroom vanity that he needed to take care of his wounds. Another thing the special ops unit taught its members. And one they hated to use because it meant they'd gotten caught or careless.

He stripped down to his boxers—white with a happy face on the front—not briefs like most women expected. His "boys" liked a bit of room to breathe. The wound on both his arm and thigh still bled sluggishly, the skin all around stained in dried blood. He held up the bottle of antiseptic and took a deep breath before pouring it on the wounds. It burned like a bastard, but he gritted his teeth as he grabbed a pair of tweezers and went after the bullet in his leg first. It took only a little digging before he plucked out the mashed piece of metal and let it plink into the sink.

It surprised him to see it was made of regular metal instead of silver. Silver weakened a shifter's immune system, and yet the mastermind's troops rarely seemed to use it. With one bullet left to dig out, he'd ponder the why later.

Unfortunately, the other wound on his upper arm proved harder to reach, and despite the various angles he tried, he couldn't dislodge the metal.

"Fucking hell." He cursed out loud as he flung the tweezers into the sink.

"What are you doing?" a slurred voice asked.

Mason pivoted to see Jessie leaning in the doorframe of his bathroom, her eyes still glazed from the drugs. "Hey, if it isn't the swan princess back in the land of the living. I see you've worked off the drugs in those cookies."

"You!" She raised a finger and pointed it in his direction, then to the left, and then the right. Her eyes blinked. "Stop moving."

"I'm not. It's the sedative still messing with you."

"I knew that. Oh. I remember what I wanted to say. I told you so."

"About the cookies?" He smiled at her triumphant, if somewhat loopy look. "Yes, you did. I am humbled before your magnificent and accurate deduction. Now, why don't you go make yourself comfortable for a minute while I finish wrapping these up?"

Her eyes dilated before narrowing in focus. Lips tight, she took in the hole in his arm, thigh, and then his bloody tools alongside the stained cloths on the counter.

"You were shot," she stated.

"'Tis but a flesh wound," he said, quoting some old Monty Python. He and his brother used to watch them over and over.

She glared at him. "Really?" She poked the hole in his arm and he yelped. "Idiot. You've got a hole in your freakn' arm. Why didn't you go to Doctor Brewster to get yourself checked out and stitched up?"

He shrugged. "My place was closer, and besides, I had a snoring princess to take care of."

"I do not snore."

"If you say so, Ms. Snorts-alot. Now, if you're done mocking my wounds and feeble bear brain, mind letting me finish this?"

A heavy sigh escaped her. "Sit down."

His brow creased. "Why?"

"So I can hurt you of course," she sassed, a ghost of a smile crossing her lips. He leaned away and her grin widened. "Pussy. I'm not going to intentionally hurt you, tempting as it sounds. But removing the bullet is likely to get a tad uncomfortable."

"I can take it. I'm a *big* bear, you know." He winked and let his meaning sink in. Bad idea. She slapped his injured arm.

"Can't you ever be serious?"

"What? I was just telling the truth. Wanna see?"

A long-suffering sigh escaped her and she stared heavenwards, muttering, "Why me?"

"Because—"

She interrupted him. "No. Don't say it. I'm sure it will just be something dirty again and I'm not in the mood. Hand me those tweezers before I lose my nerve."

"You don't have to do this," he said softly, noticing how she swallowed hard and took shallow breaths when she focused on his wound again.

"I'm a big girl. I can do this, but just so you know, I don't like blood."

"Is that a warning you might faint and need me to catch you?"

"No, more a forewarning that I might throw up and it will probably land in your lap."

The expression on his face surely didn't merit the loud laughter that spewed from her. He tried to glare at her in return, but truly, in that moment, her face alight with humor, her lips curved in a wide smile, and her eyes shining lucidly finally, he'd never thought her more beautiful.

He sat down on the toilet, not exactly the most noble seating arrangement, and decided he could handle any chunks that came his way if it meant she'd touch him. But just in case, he didn't close the lid to the bowl and spread his legs, praying her aim was true.

Hesitant fingers touched his arm, and he peered at her, loving how she sucked in her bottom lip as she gazed with consternation at his wound.

"You saved me." She said it as a statement rather than a question, and he nodded.

"As soon as I saw you'd eaten the cookies, I went looking for you. I almost didn't make it in time." The knowledge of how close he'd come to losing her chilled him still and he shivered.

"You're cold. I'll try and hurry." Hands shaking, she lightly touched his injury.

"I'll live," he said dryly. "You don't have to do this. I'll eventually get the sucker out myself." With her shaking hand, it might prove less painful and damaging if he did it himself.

"I can do this," she muttered, bending to the task, her face close enough to send her breath fluttering across his skin.

He couldn't help the burgeoning interest from his cock any more than he could stop from inhaling, letting her warm, citrusy scent wash over him.

Basking in the pleasure of her closeness, he didn't even flinch when she poked the hole in his arm with the tweezers. Didn't let out a sound when she clumsily probed at his wound, although he did grit his teeth. She eventually tore the offending metal piece free with an exclamation of, "Got it!" Her triumphant smile made her painful surgery worth it, a pleasure that quickly dwindled as the savage princess then swabbed him with antiseptic and grabbed a needle.

"Um, I don't think that's necessary," he said as she closed one eye, the tip of her pink tongue peeking as she tried to thread the hole in the deadly-looking pin.

"Don't be such a baby bear."

"Is this your way of telling me you have a lot of experience sewing things?" he asked, doubt in his tone.

"I'm a princess. I've never darned a thing in my life, but there's no time like the present," she said with a bright smile. She dropped to her knees, and peered up at him with a mischievous grin. "I'm sure this won't hurt too much."

So cute, and with that one look, up went his

dick again.

She poised her hand with the needle over his thigh and looked down. He knew when she noticed his happy state because her eyes widened and her mouth dropped open.

"Going to take care of my other problem too?" he teased.

"And to think I felt sorry for you," she growled, stabbing his skin with the needle, then wincing at his yelp.

He placed his hand over hers. "I think I'll stick with the spray on bandage if you don't mind."

"Suit yourself." She stood and handed him the spray bottle before walking out. Sure, she appeared pissed, but he smiled anyway because despite her annoyance, he knew one thing for sure. She wanted him. The smell of it tickled his senses and made him hurry to finish cleaning up, because now that he'd gotten her back to his cave, he wasn't about to let her go. Even the temptation hidden in a stolen picnic basket didn't excite him as much as the thought of touching or tasting her did. Campers everywhere would rejoice.

* * * *

Jessie paced the living room decorated in earthy tones but with a modern contemporary feel. So many emotions swirled through her. Relief Mason had saved her. Chagrin at his injury. Arousal at his half-naked state. And most of all, annoyance, because despite all the reasons not to, despite her words to him earlier, he obviously still desired her, and damn him, she wanted him too.

Which was why she needed to leave. Now. Thankfully, she eschewed purses so she had a pocketful of cash and her keys, not that she made it far. The only door, which doubled as an elevator, wouldn't open.

"It's key card activated," he supplied from much too close behind her.

She whirled and noted he wore some loose pants, hiding at least part of him, but that still left her with way too much bare chest to stare at. Focusing on the dark hairs that curled upon its surface didn't help tamp her budding arousal, rather it enflamed it. She poked his rock hard pec in the hopes he'd move back.

"Mind giving me some space?"

He stepped closer.

"What do you think you are doing?" she snapped.

"I was ordered to stick close to you in case the kidnapping attempt was intentional."

"I doubt it. Now open this door so I can go home."

"No." He brushed up against her, and despite how firmly she pressed against the barrier behind her, she couldn't escape the heat and hardness of him.

"What do you mean no? You can't just keep me here."

"Actually, I can."

"I'll call Kloe."

"Who will back me up because your safety is of utmost importance."

"I'll-I'll call my dad."

Mason's breath fluttered against her temple before he rubbed his lips across it. "I doubt you'd sink that low. Or do you really want to be married to that uptight stick your dad has chosen?"

No, but still... She couldn't stay here.

Couldn't stay here and let those lips of his traveling down the side of her face go any further. She needed to stop this madness. Mason was a womanizer. He'd fuck her and leave her. Worse, he'd probably show her so much pleasure he'd ruin her for any other man, not that she wanted any other man. Not like she wanted Mason.

"This is wrong," she whispered as his mouth trailed across the edge of her jaw.

"If it's wrong then why does it feel so right?" he murmured before claiming her mouth.

Then she forgot why she needed to keep him at a distance. Didn't care if he only wanted her for a quick romp. Didn't give a damn if her father expected her to marry a stranger or that she'd probably regret this in the morning. All she wanted was more. More of Mason. More of the heated pleasure that wanted to erupt so badly in her body.

Screw the consequences. She'd gotten kidnapped and almost ended up as a monkey in some madman's lab. She deserved a moment of bliss to remember she lived. And Mason deserved a prize for saving her.

She wrapped her arms around him, and pressed her mouth back against his, a fierceness entering her kiss that proved contagious as his mouth went from soft and coaxing to hard and demanding. The heated passion of it stole her breath, leaving her panting, her mouth opening at the probing insistence of his tongue. A wet duel ensued as their tongues twined in a sinuous dance that she felt all the way to her toes. But it was her cleft that enjoyed it the most, moistening and quivering as an aching need built in her.

Turning wild under his embrace, the next thing she knew, she whirled them, swapping positions so she could push him back against the wall, hungrily taking control of the kiss. Never before had she acted so aggressively. So needy. She wanted to devour every inch of him. Taste the taut skin that had tempted her for weeks. She tore her mouth from his and placed hot kisses on the hollow of his neck.

He groaned, and his hands, palming her buttocks, squeezed, eliciting a sound of pleasure from her. She nuzzled her face against the fuzz of his chest, rubbing her cheek against it before swooping to bite down on one of his flat nipples. He growled and she chuckled as she tugged his flesh.

"Like it a little rough?" she teased him as she nipped him again, loving how his hips surged forward to grind against her covered cleft.

"Maybe." He spun her so her back once again leaned against the wall. His dark eyes bored into hers as he let his hands find the hem of her long shirt and tug it up until his hands touched the bare skin of her waist. Where his hands traveled, skimming across skin, he left a trail of fire, and she lifted her arms without him asking so that he could take the shirt right off her. A certain amount of shyness overcame her as he stared at her abundant cleavage and rounded belly. Her white bra stood out in stark contrast to her skin, but if his ardent gaze was any indication, he liked what he saw.

"So delicious-looking," he murmured, dipping his head. He kissed the valley between her breasts as his hands cupped her heavy globes, squeezing them.

Her breathing hitched when he caught her nipple in his mouth, fabric and all, the scorching heat of his mouth not impeded at all by the flimsy lace in his way. Grasping his head, she tugged at his hair, drawing him closer, growling softly as he inhaled her breast into his mouth, as much as he could manage.

I need him The urgent desire to have him inside of her pussy, pounding her flesh, made use her grip on his scalp to pull him up. He made a sound of protest that died when she brought her hands to the waistband of his track pants and pushed them down. She made sure to drag his boxers with them, letting his cock spring forth, long and thick to slap against the skin of her belly. She wrapped her hands around his length, loving how he hissed and bucked his hips at her quick strokes. As she continued to caress him, pumping his shaft, fascinated at the contrast of her skin against his, he got busy, his hands finding and unbuckling her own pants, their looseness allowing them to fall down over her hips with ease. She didn't let go of him as she kicked off her boots and stepped out of her cargo pants, tugging him hard and laughing softly at his strangled moan of pleasure. A moan she repeated when his hand found its way between her thighs. He growled softly, a sexy rumble that made him vibrate, when he discovered her damp panties.

One fleeting touch and she almost lost it. She pumped his cock faster, her hips jerking in time to the motion of her hand.

"If you don't stop, this is going to be embarrassingly short," he groaned.

"Ha, like I haven't seen that before," she retorted, still too fascinated by his girth and feel to stop.

But her words got an unexpected reaction. The next thing she knew, her hands were pinned above her head and his body pressed against hers—naked, hot skin that felt oh so good—while his gaze blazed down, boring into her.

"I am not one of those other guys. And while this first time might be a little quick, I can promise you, by the end of this night, you won't just forget all those other inept boys, you'll never want anyone else."

Exactly what she feared. For a moment, doubt about her actions assailed her, but as if reading her mind, Mason gripped her tighter, his mouth almost punishing in its kiss. As he devoured her mouth, he used one of his hands to clamp both of hers together. The other traveled down her body to her hip. A rip of fabric parting preceded him peeling her panties from her. Caught under his erotic spell, she parted her thighs at the insistent probing of his fingers. She expected him to go for the gold like experience dictated, for once she actually wanted it, but instead, he cupped her. It should have felt odd, or stupid, but the heat of his palm made her hotter and she arched into his touch, silently asking for more. He dragged a finger through her folds, wetting it on her desire before circling around her nub. She wanted to protest his slow torture, but his mouth had effectively captured hers, preventing any sound from escaping.

And then he touched her. Rubbed his slick finger against her clit in a rapid back and forth motion. Made her body hum like never before. Given her already heightened state of arousal, it was enough to make her come, her cries of rapture captured by his mouth. When he let go of her hands to grab her by the waist and hoist her, she thought herself done, and just figured she'd endure while he went along for his own ride. But as soon as the tip of his cock pressed against her still quivering sex, a shudder went through her, and she discovered she wanted him inside her. Wanted him to stretch her and claim her.

She wrapped her legs around his flanks, trying to draw him into her body. But he held back, easing himself in with an agonizing slowness that made the cords in his neck stand out and had her whimpering in need. When he finally sheathed himself fully, she let out a long moan, loving how he filled her and how her flesh clamped around him so tight. She didn't think it could feel any better until he started to move, short, swirling strokes that made her arousal of just moments before seem like nothing as pleasure hit her hard and fast, bringing her to the edge of bliss with almost insane rapidity.

His hands slid from her waist to grasp her buttocks, his fingers digging into her fleshy cheeks as he thrust faster and faster into her, their bodies slick with sweat. In and out, each deep stroke made her cry out until she came again, an overwhelming wave of pleasure that had her screaming his name as she clutched him to her tightly.

He yelled himself when he climaxed, his body thrusting one last time into hers, a warm gush of liquid heat that made her shudder as the aftershocks kept sweeping through her.

Limp as a noodle, and drowsy to boot, she didn't protest when he carried them to bed, their bodies still intimately entwined. Heck, she didn't even move away when he crawled into bed beside her, his big body spooning around hers. Instead of doing anything, like getting dressed and leaving, or shoving him away as she usually would, she fell asleep with a smile on her lips, and an unexpected warmth in her heart.

Chapter Seven

Mason woke with dozens of plans crowding his mind, all of them involving ways of making Jessie scream his name in pleasure again. *I can't believe I fell asleep after that mind-blowing experience.* He'd planned to make love to her all night long. A matter he'd rectify shortly.

Elated that he'd finally gotten to make love to his chocolate princess, he was understandably miffed when he not only woke with a pounding headache, but to the fact he was no longer in his bedroom. As if fucking up his chances of morning sex with his irresistible swan lady weren't enough, his kidnappers had handcuffed him, with silver no less, spread eagle in a cell, stark freaking naked. Not that his body was a thing to be ashamed of. In tip-top shape, and hung like a bear—which was impressive for those who only seemed to ever compare to horses—he didn't have a problem with nudity per se, on his terms. Having someone capture him while he slept, and chain him up, pissed him off.

None of his feelings compared, though, to his rage when he saw Jessie in the same situation in the next cell over. *Who dared touched my bird?* He roared, fury making him snap, and bringing forth his bear in a skin-splitting second. His beast, stronger and thicker than his human shape, easily snapped the manacles holding him—more like tore them from the cement wall in a cacophony of screaming metal. He snarled as he headed for the bars of his cage, one need foremost in his mind. *Saving my female.* Oh and covering her from possibly spying eyes. That naked skin belonged to him and him alone.

He grasped the bars, prepared to bend them, and a jolt went through him that shook his entire body. The smell of singed fur tickled his nostrils. It took Jessie screaming his name for him to release the bars and stare at his scorched hands. Ouch.

Fuckers. They'd electrified the bars. What did they take him for? An animal? In that case, the laws of the wild would apply, which meant killing and maiming were definitely on the menu. He roared in challenge.

"Hey, Smokey, mind losing the rabid act for a minute."

He heard Jessie's soft chastisement and lifted a shaggy head only to gaze in frustrated agony at Jessie, who struggled in her own set of chains. *How could I have been so careless?* Because he blamed himself for their current situation. He should have run with Jessie, taken her some place far where no one would have gotten their hands, or paws, on her. Instead, he'd let his cock rule his mind, and made love to her before collapsing into what he now suspected was an unnatural slumber. The only thing he couldn't figure out was how they found them. Mason didn't keep his address on file anywhere. As a matter of fact, the name on his condo, as well as all the utilities, were under that of a corporation to make him almost impossible to find. And he knew for a fact no one followed them to his place. So how did they locate them and manage to drug them? And more important, where exactly did Jessie sit in regards to him this morning?

Needing to talk to her, he shifted back to his human body.

"Sorry for losing control there. I am understandably annoyed. Are you okay?" he asked.

She stopped her thrashing to give him an incredulous look. "Did you seriously just ask me that? I am chained, naked I might add, in a fucking cell and you want to know if I'm okay?"

He shrugged and fought the heat that wanted to rise in his cheeks. She had a point, but what else could he say? *Hey the sex was fantastic last night, and by the way, sorry for falling asleep before showing you nirvana a half dozen more times. Oh and sorry too for falling victim to a trap to snag us both.* It galled him that someone had penetrated his condo in the first place. It pissed him off even more that he'd slept through the entire fucking thing. His sergeant would have strung up his ass for such a lapse. Castigation wouldn't help them, though. Well, unless Jessie wielded the whip. Bad bear. He needed to get his mind out of the gutter. His swan princess needed his help.

"Okay, I'll admit, the situation is a little dire. Don't worry. I'll figure something out. I'm a master at escape."

"Gee, seeing how well your first plan worked, I'm feeling so much better already," she replied sarcastically with a glance at his burning hands.

Damn, but she knew how to use that tongue. He hid the evidence of his injuries behind his back.

Out of sight, out of mind. "Would it help if I said you look hot in those chains?" He smiled. She glared. Some things never changed. But, really, she did look pretty sweet with her full breasts jiggling as she struggled, her outstretched arms exposing them nicely. A man could do so many things to a body strung up and ready for feasting.

"Can you get your brain out of your dick long enough to figure out a way to get us out of here?"

He peeked down at his cock, and sure enough, even though the situation appeared grave, someone was happy to see Jessie naked and awake. It would probably help if he could stop staring at her body, but damn, what a hard task, especially now that he knew of the passion lurking under her cold exterior.

"How do you know this isn't part of my plan to help us escape?" he asked, arching his hips to point his erection at the bars. He waggled it for good measure.

"Oh Mason, thank God for your *massive* weapon of destruction," she simpered. Then smirked. "Are you telling me you have magical jizz hiding in your balls that's suddenly going to melt the bars and help us escape?"

"Oh it's magical all right, baby. Swallow it and you'll see." He leered in an exaggerated fashion, hoping for a smile.

She sighed in resignation. "We are never going to escape, are we?"

"There you go with that negativity again. Funny, last night, you had no problem screaming 'Yes!'"

Was that a blush making her cheeks bloom? Oh yes, and it went well with the vague scent of arousal that tickled his nose.

"Last night was a one-time thing. You got your rocks off. I scratched my itch. Now can we change the subject?"

An itch? She compared her two screaming orgasms to a rude bodily need? He leaned back against the wall and crossed his arms over his chest. "No. I want to discuss last night. Because whether you choose to believe it or not, we are going to make love again. And again. In a lot of different positions."

"Oh no we're not. You got what you wanted. Time to move on."

"Nope. I'm looking forward to a repeat of last night. As a matter of fact, I see us spending a lot of time, naked, together." Because he'd discovered something in the week he'd tried to avoid his ornery swan princess. He needed her and for more than just one night.

"There is no *us*," she hissed. "Last night was an aberration. A thank you, I guess, for saving me."

"Well, if that's how you're going to say thanks, I'd better get cracking on rescuing you again. You might want to get yourself ready for me over there. I don't plan on this taking long."

"Do you ever take anything seriously?"

He let his lips stretch in a slow smile. "Oh, I take the task of getting you screaming my name again while you claw my back very seriously."

"I told you that won't happen again."

"Yes, it will."

She pursed her lips. "You are so freakn' stubborn."

"People who live in glass houses shouldn't throw stones," he taunted.

"You're a bear. I'm a bird. Some species really shouldn't mix."

"I disagree. I think variety is great for a relationship."

"Really? And what are you basing that assumption on?"

"You want a prime example? Chase is quite happy with his bunny."

"A killer bunny. Me, I'm just a nerdy swan, one step away from becoming a stuffed Butterball dinner."

"I've got something to stuff you with." He smirked as he gyrated his hips, drawing her gaze down. He gave his hard dick an extra wiggle.

Her head shot up and she gaped incredulously at him. "Keep your dirty thoughts and cock away from my pie."

"Mmm. Did you have to remind me of how edible you are? I never did get a chance to have a taste." He waggled his tongue at her and she hissed in frustration. Damn, but even given the situation, he was having loads of fun baiting his princess.

"You're impossible."

"Want us to kill him?" The query came from a new voice, one Mason recognized as the gun-toting hyena of the day before.

"You!" Mason approached the bars, careful not to touch them as he stared daggers at the dirty thug who'd managed to capture them.

"Yes, me. I have to say, the mastermind was most miffed when you didn't use the attack as an excuse to run to your brother and his wife. We'd really hoped you were as stupid as you look."

"You'll never find Chase and Miranda," he

boasted. Not that he knew their location, but knowing Victor, he'd hidden them well.

The hyena shrugged and smiled. Not a reassuring look, not with the mad glint in its eyes. "Maybe not yet, but instead of worrying about them, shouldn't you be wondering what's going to happen to you?"

Not really. Mason wasn't exactly in a hurry to find out because, somehow, he doubted he'd like it. "Why don't you get in here and show me?" A toothy smile went well with his challenge. However, a high-pitched raucous laugh was the thug's response.

"You'd like that, wouldn't you? I have a better idea, though. Why don't I wander into your girlfriend's cage? I hear she's a screamer. Shall we test that knowledge?"

"Come near me and I will bite something off," Jessie spat.

"You'll be too busy screaming," the hyena said, withdrawing a syringe from its pocket. "See, even without that stupid werebunny's blood, we've come up with a prototype. Of course, finding testing subjects has gotten harder. So many of them die. Or go insane, making it hard to gauge success."

"Don't you fucking dare." Mason's low threat emerged stark and cold. He'd gone past fury right into icy fear.

"And how are you going to stop me?" With a giggle that bordered on insane, the hyena approached Jessie, who struggled anew to release herself, fear making her eyes wide as the needle drew closer.

Snap. The sound of Mason losing his mind was almost audible. He changed forms in an instant and rushed the bars, slamming his body into them, ignoring the sizzling pain of the electricity that burned across his skin. *Bang!* He bear-rushed the bars again, denting the metal. But while he had yet to escape, the hyena at least paused in its dastardly approach.

Unable to articulate himself in this form, Mason nevertheless growled, a low, ominous rumble that bared his sharp teeth. Again, he slammed the cage until the hyena turned to face him instead with the deadly needle filled with its experimental fluid.

But Mason didn't care. Not if it saved his Jessie. He prepared to rush the bars again when a commotion at the door drew all their attention. A humanoid scurried in, his nose twitching.

"Boss. We've been found. The eagles are landing."

The what? Mason surely wore the same puzzled expression the hyena did.

"What the fuck are you babbling about? The eagle shifters are extinct."

"Well tell that to the giant white birds dropping from the sky," snapped the subordinate.

"Oh fuck. Daddy's here." The disgust in Jessie's voice surprised him. He glanced over at her and saw her close her eyes, her lips moving as she muttered under her breath.

"Bloody hell." The hyena cursed as he stalked toward the door, his minion scattering before him. But just before he left, he turned and with a malicious smile said, "Oh, wait. I think I forgot something."

Quicker than the human eye could have followed, the thug tossed the syringe like a dart, a single fluorescent green drop hanging from its tip. It flew with unerring accuracy through the bars to hit

Jessie in the thigh. And even though the plunger wasn't pressed, she screamed.

Oh God, did she scream.

The insane laughter of the hyena as it left barely registered over the sound of Mason once again battering at his cage walls. He broke free in a sizzle of fur of skin and was about to hit the bars caging Jessie when a sharp prick hit him between the shoulder blades, followed by a half dozen more.

Roaring, he meant to whirl on the bastards who dared attack him from behind, but lethargy seeped through his limbs. *Shit. Drugged again.* As he slumped to the ground in slow motion, he held out a furry paw toward Jessie, the agony in her glazed eyes the most painful thing he'd ever experienced and the focal point of his nightmare.

Chapter Eight

The second time she woke up not knowing where she was proved a touch better than the first. Jessie blinked at the vividly white ceiling above her and let her aching body enjoy the soft mattress beneath her. Unfettered and smelling clean, she briefly wondered where she lay until she noticed the familiar emblem carved into the post of the bed. Her father's house—more like mansion—although not the room she grew up in, probably because in a fit of rage at her refusal to tow the line, her dear old dad had it remade into a theater room. Jessie thought the dark room was a marked improvement over the sterile white of most of the other spaces in the house. Her dad seriously lacked imagination when it came to décor.

Location solved, she allowed herself to think back on the last moment she recalled. Not fun because it involved pain, lots of it, and a really pissed off brown bear. Forget Yogi. Mason in his shifted form was the type of bear park rangers warned campers to stay away from. Jessie, however, wouldn't have minded getting closer because the whole rabid bear act came about because of the danger she found herself in. A danger Mason obviously wanted to protect her from. How cute. How wrong. How confusing.

But she'd think on her emotions for the bear—

and his fabulous love-making—later. As she recalled, that hyena in need of a neck adjustment—broken being preferred—had stuck her with a needle, which contained some deadly serum, or so he implied. Worried, she sat up in the bed and checked herself over. Arms, legs, hands, feet, all seemed normal. Her skin color appeared the same. Her face? She popped off the bed, the white nightie someone placed on her reaching only mid-thigh, and hunted for a mirror, which she found in the ensuite bathroom. Peering at herself anxiously in the reflective surface, she sighed when she didn't see any signs of a third eye, or bulges indicating tumors, or extra limbs trying to grow.

It seemed whatever the hyena intended to dose her with was either needed in greater concentrations or a dud. Either way, other than a little soreness in her muscles, she felt fine.

What about Mason, though? She wondered how he'd healed from his injuries. Even in the mess surrounding them, she'd not missed the burns on his body as he slammed the cage trying to escape in a crazy effort to rescue her. She needed to find him.

Not because her heart hammered in her chest with worry. Not because her body tingled in anticipation for more of his touch. And certainly not because she liked him. No way. Uh-uh. She went looking for him to make sure he got the care he deserved. Nothing else. *Liar.*

She'd bitch slap herself later for the deceit. Right now, she owned a burning need to know his fate.

Forget making it out the door, though. It swung open before she reached it and her father stalked in with a foul look on his face—not to be mistaken with fowl, which was how he looked when shifted. Her mind giggled insanely. Still, no matter which "F" word she contemplated, either way his presence created an instant remission in her recovery. She sank onto the bed, and prepared for the diatribe.

"You're awake. Excellent." His false joviality didn't fool her for an instant.

"I'm feeling fine. Thanks for asking." Sarcasm just couldn't be helped around her father.

"I see your tongue is in fine form. That will make the priest happy."

"Priest? What priest? Am I dying? Is he coming to give me last rites?" For a moment, she worried, wondering what she'd missed.

"You are not dying, although you almost did working for that inept agency. You can bet my lawyers will be serving them their asses on a platter."

"It wasn't their fault," she defended.

"No? Then whose was it? The bear's? I've got a special punishment planned for him."

"Mason's alive?"

"The overgrown carnivore lives. For now," he said ominously.

Her heart thumped in her chest at her father's threat. "You leave Mason out of it. He tried to save me."

"His carelessness, not to mention your lack of common sense, is what got you in trouble in the first place."

"What are you talking about?"

"A bear? Really, Jessica? I realize it is your goal in life to embarrass the family, but if you feel a need to fornicate out of wedlock, couldn't you at least stick to your own kind?"

"You mean fuck Eric instead?" She loved how her crude words made her father's lips tighten. "I'd rather gang bang one of each species first." Not, but she enjoyed the lie. It made her father's white skin turn such a brilliant shade of red.

"I swear, if I hadn't had the DNA test done myself, I would wonder whose egg you hatched from."

She would have taken offense, except she'd had the same test repeated—twice—just to make sure. So much for her changeling theory. She'd often hoped growing up that she truly was an ugly duckling disguised as a swan princess. "Gee, don't smother me in love there, Dad. I might just choke. Anyway, fascinating as our talk is, I've got to get going. Things to do. People to see. Bears to bang. You know. Fun stuff."

The icy smile that crossed her dad's lips did nothing to warm her. Actually, given the triumphant glint in his eye, it sent a shiver through her body. "There is only one thing you are doing when you step through that door and it involves a priest, a visiting prince, and you saying yes when prompted."

The startled honk that came from her throat just made her father's grin widen. "Not fucking likely," she snapped. "I've put up with this charade long enough. Either you tell Eric the engagement is off, or I will. And if you keep pushing it, I will end it in a public fashion that will embarrass you for all time."

"Disobey, and a certain bear in the dungeon will turn into a coat for your Aunt Matilda."

Shock made her gasp. "You wouldn't dare!"

"Try me. Your lover has already caused me enough aggravation."

Good for Mason. "You can't do this. We are not living in the dark ages, Dad. And you can't force me into a shotgun wedding."

"I can and will."

"No, you won't." The quiet yet firm claim came from Eric, who stood framed in the doorway wearing jeans and a t-shirt. She blinked at his casual attire, a first that actually made him look…decent.

"She's just got cold feet," her father claimed. "She'll get over it. Shouldn't you be dressed already, though? We are about to start the ceremony."

"No, we aren't." Again with the firm certainty. Despite the situation, Jessie almost started to like the guy. But not enough to marry him. "I put up with this farce because my mom made me promise. Lucky for me, though, my mother actually loves me, and after seeing how much I disliked the thought of marrying for position instead of at least affection, she released me from my vow. Princess." Eric bowed in her direction, his clear blue gaze briefly meeting hers. "I release you from our engagement and wish you well in life."

"Thank you." She said the words softly.

"You're welcome." A rueful smile graced his lips. "I have to wonder if under other circumstances, perhaps things would have developed differently."

"Maybe. Good flight."

"And to you too, princess." With another short bow, the visiting prince left.

Unfortunately, her father didn't.

"Oh that's just great," her father honked, his agitation ruffling his hair. "Exactly how am I supposed to explain there's not going to be a wedding?"

"Not my problem. Maybe if you took the time to listen to your family once in a while instead of dictating, these types of things wouldn't happen."

A dangerous glint entered her father's eyes. "This is all your fault. If you'd shown Eric the least encouragement, he would have never broken things off. But no, you'd rather taint yourself with the touch of a wild animal. Well, so be it. You like the bear so much, then I hope you can stand him forever. Guards!"

Incomprehension made her frown when her father's burly guards entered. Swans on steroids were never a pretty sight in either their human or bird form. When they grabbed her arms, she still didn't quite know what her father meant to do.

"You're disowning me finally?" she queried, secretly hoping the answer was yes.

"No."

"Throwing me out?"

"No."

"Putting me in the dungeon?"

"Try again. This time, though, think wedding bells and a bear."

Wedding and… Her eyes widened. "You can't make me wed Mason."

"Why not? He was good enough to fornicate with. Since you prefer him over your own kind, then why not make it permanent?"

"You can't do this," she yelled as the guards lifted her via her arms off her feet. "Mason will never agree."

"Did I say he had a choice? Neither of you do,

unless you prefer death."

"Death for what reason?" she spat.

"Ah, but you see, by consorting with the bear and in turn causing our pending alliance with the Canadians to fail, you have performed treason against the flock."

"You're insane."

"No, I'm king, something you seem to have forgotten. Although, once you marry the beast, who I am won't matter as theirs is a matriarchal based society. Hope his mama bear likes you else you're likely to become dinner."

And with those final words, her dad left her while she screamed, mostly nasty, vile things that she'd see done to him.

However, all the yelling in the world didn't stop the guards from carrying her bodily down the stairs into a throne room filled with guests. And to her eternal embarrassment, all eyes turned her way.

So she did what she usually did when in situations that made her uncomfortable—or pissed her off—she flipped them the bird.

* * * *

Gnawing on a bone in the corner of a dark dungeon cell, unshaven, unwashed, and not too fucking happy, Mason waited for his chance to escape.

Two days by his count they'd held him prisoner. Two agonizing days of wondering how Jessie fared. Of washing his painful burns with tepid water and munching on dry bread and rancid meat. His only entertainment and extra source of protein came from the most unlikely source. The hyena, the same one who dared kidnap him and Jessie in the first place, ended up thrown in with him. His screams only lightened Mason's dark mood—and satisfied his hunger for red meat—for a short while before he paced the small confines of his prison once again.

He could have probably shifted and torn the door from its hinges and gone on a rampage that would render him infamous—among his kind at any rate. He'd probably end up reviled among the avian species, though, and it was only that fact that stayed his paw. If Jessie lived, and he prayed every single second of every single day she did, then she probably wouldn't look kindly on him stuffing, with chestnuts and bread crumbs, spitting over a fire, slowly roasting to a crispy perfection, and eating her family. Heck, since he'd met her, he now felt bad about every turkey dinner he'd enjoyed, even if those ugly gobblers thankfully never made it to the higher level of shape-shifting.

So, despite his need for answers and action, he held on to his burning rage and agony over not knowing. Bided his time while he waited because they couldn't keep him forever. A bear only had so much patience, and once they exhausted it…

The thumping of many booted feet saw him scrambling to his feet and watching the door. With a click of numerous locks, and the snick of a bar being slid out of place, the portal swung open and a feeble light penetrated the darkness, not that he needed any faint illumination to see the old guy dressed in white from head to toe, buttressed by buff guards. Even freakier than the guy's pristine apparel, buddy's flesh just about blended in to his outfit so pale was his skin and hair. Judging by the golden crown atop his head, Mason deduced he was about to finally meet Jessie's dad, the swan king. If the tight lips and irritated eyes of the avian monarch were any indication, they wouldn't get along.

"So you're the disgusting beast my daughter's been consorting with. Appalling."

"Funny, I would have said I'm a step up from her boring fiancé."

"Ex fiancé," snapped the king. "Because of you, the prince has broken off the engagement and left."

Mason couldn't stop his smile from blossoming. "Well, happy birthday to me."

"You think that's a good thing? Ignorant bear. You should have kept your dirty paws to yourself."

"Now why would I do that when Jessie enjoys them so much?" Okay, it was bad of him to bait the old bird, but seriously, the guy's picture could probably be found with a stick up his ass under the definition of uptight.

The cold smile of the swan should have warned him he'd not like his next words. "I'm glad you like my daughter so much because you're about to spend the rest of your lives together."

"Why, are you killing us and shoving us in a grave together?"

"No."

"Imprisoning her in here with me? Awesome."

That ruffled a few feathers. "No."

"Marrying us?" Mason chuckled as he threw that one out, then choked at the replied, "Yes, as a matter of fact."

Disbelief made him blurt, "Hold on a second. You mean you want us to get engaged?"

"I want more than that. Before this day ends, you and Jessie will be man and wife. Or should I say, swan and bear. A fitting reward, or should I say punishment, for your dalliance."

Uh-oh. "Jessie's not going to like that." Actually, he could already imagine her hiss of displeasure. Maybe a kick or two. Definitely some scowls.

"As if I care what a cygnet thinks. And what about you? Aren't you going to roar and beat your chest like you primitive beasts like to do, threatening me and looking for a way to escape?"

Would he? Mason put together the concept of marriage with his image of Jessie, along with his burgeoning feelings of the last month and an erotic visual of her flushed face as he made love to her. The result? "Why would I protest? I love your daughter." By damn, did he ever. It was a wonder it took him this long to clue in to what his feelings represented. "And besides, who am I to argue a free wedding and food? There is going to be food right, Dad?" His tummy rumbled right on queue.

Was it the insouciance of his reply or his nickname for the swan king that made him turn that wicked shade of red? Mason didn't really care because he was going to marry a swan princess. And not just any princess. His Jessie. Boy, was she going to be pissed, but not as pissed as his mama when she discovered she'd not gotten invited to the wedding.

Chapter Nine

Jessie stopped struggling to escape the guards once they reached the altar covered in white linen and white roses set up on the dais. She had to when she noticed each thrash of her legs showed off her undies to the gathered flock who cackled likes hens—*stupid bird brains*—to each other.

How embarrassing. Not just her state of dishabille, but her father's treatment. Funny how he accused her of humiliating him at every turn and yet he was the one who kept pulling shit like this. Marry her bear indeed. As if her dad would follow through. Even he didn't have the balls—no, seriously, he didn't—to actually enforce his threat. But that didn't mean he was done with her, or poor Mason yet.

Despite not knowing what would happen, she couldn't deny a certain anticipation over seeing her bear again. It galled her to admit she missed and worried about the giant furball. When had he managed to creep under her thick skin and make her care about him? The jerk.

Patience was not one of her strong suits and as the minutes ticked by without either her father or Mason appearing, she wondered what held her dad up. *Did he change his mind? Did he tell Mason of his insane plan to marry us? Did Mason lose his mind and kill him? Did...*

Eve Langlais

The myriad questions and concerns swirling in her head couldn't have prepared her for the reality. Striding free of guards and encumbrance, Mason appeared through the giant arched doors at the far end of the room. Dressed in a white suit that he must have borrowed, his face clean shaven, his head held high, he looked delicious. No, wait, she meant to think healthy and safe. No, sexy and delicious were much more appropriate, she revised as he strode down the aisle, cocky confidence in every step, his lips stretched in a wide grin that turned into a glower as he took note of the guards that held her arms in viselike grips.

When he reached the bottom of the dais, he growled, "Let her go before I eat you." The menace in his tone just made the idiots holding her clamp down harder and she winced. Mason took a step forward, his lip curling back in a snarl. Despite the potential for bloodshed, she found it rather hot.

"Do as the bear says." Her father's voice snapped from behind the throne. He stepped into view, a scowl on his face. Not unusual, actually, and neither were the icy daggers his eyes threw. It was the recipient that surprised her. For once, her father didn't try to kill her with his gaze. Instead, Mason bore the brunt. And the big, hairy idiot smiled even wider.

"Mason," she hissed. "You've got to escape before my dad unleashes his evil plan."

"Evil? There's nothing evil about wanting to join a man and a woman together in holy matrimony," her father replied, still continuing his charade.

"Enough with the games, Father. You've

108

embarrassed the family enough at this point, don't you think?"

"I've embarrassed?" her dad said in a mocking voice. "I'm not the one taking carnivores as lovers."

"Maybe you should. After all, only a meat eater can really know how to eat co—"

Jessie elbowed Mason in the stomach before he could finish. Too late. The shocked hush indicated the crowd had already filled in the blank.

"Insolent bear!"

If worry for Mason didn't have her in its grips, she would have enjoyed the purple shade her father turned.

"Ignore him, Dad. He's got impulse control problems." She scrambled to find a way to divert her father's attention. "I'm the one you're mad at. Remember? Rebellious daughter. Black swan of the family." Literally.

Cold eyes perused her. "I thank the great lord that your mother didn't live to see the day her daughter brought such shame to her lineage. At least by marrying you to this creature, it will keep the taint away from the flock. Let the ceremony start."

She gaped at her father as the elderly pastor, his bill mottled with age, tottered to the dais. "You can't do this. Your problem is with me, not him. Let him go."

"It became his problem when he seduced you."

"But people have sex all the time. It doesn't mean you force them to marry," she sputtered.

"Princesses are supposed to remain chaste," her father spat. "Bad enough you couldn't wait for wedlock. By fornicating with the four-legged beast, you sealed your fate. Priest, marry them."

Panicked, she turned to face Mason, apology in her gaze. Big brown eyes caught hers, the look in Mason's gaze warming her instantly, but not as much as his hand when it engulfed hers and drew her close to his body. "Don't worry, baby," he rumbled in a low tone. "I've got this under control." He winked, and she relaxed.

If she could trust anyone to get them out of this mess—AKA farce of a wedding—then it would be Mason, the playbear. He'd never allow himself to become shackled to one woman for life.

She kept that belief through the quickly rendered ceremony, and it wasn't until she heard Mason say, "I do," that doubt niggled her. *When will his plan kick in?*

The priest prompted her to reply, and she peeked at Mason. He gave her a nod of his head and a smile. Trusting in him, she whispered, "I do."

"Then by the power vested in me, I now pronounce you swan and bear. You may kiss your bird."

Familiar bulky arms wrapped around her and leaned her upper body back. Before she could say a word, his lips claimed hers in a hot embrace that stole all reason from her. But what he stole in sanity, he returned in heat, the molten kind that went winding through her whole body, setting her aflame. She forgot where she was. What had just happened. Heck, she wasn't sure if she remembered her name in that moment. However, she did know she wanted more. Her hands crept around his neck as she returned his tender kiss, and she would have slipped him some tongue if not for the rude honk that separated her from Mason.

Her father glared at her. "Unbelievable."

"No, incredible," Mason drawled. "And later on it will probably be phenomenal and loud. Very loud. And probably more than twice. No, make that three times."

Jessie blinked as she tried to filter his words, but gave up on replying when she finally understood, embarrassment rendering her mute. Mason, though, owned no such shame. Still clutching her tight to his side, he beamed like a bear having the time of his life. Jessie could only emit a strangled moan when he said, "Hey, Dad, didn't you say this shindig was going to have some food? I need some energy for later, if you know what I mean." The wink was probably the last straw.

As exits went, theirs was quite prompt, but not rough. Mason wouldn't let the guards who surrounded them to escort them out lay one wingtip on her, or him for that matter. Instead, sweeping her into his big arms—her nightie firmly tucked under her round bottom, keeping her modestly more or less intact—he strode from the castle whistling jauntily, the picture of a male well pleased with himself.

Once outside, he let her down and approached a parked car whose chauffeur leaned against it having a smoke.

"I'm hungry and in need of wheels," he stated. "So which of my needs are you going to supply?" Mason grinned and clacked his teeth.

The goose, with a honk, threw his keys at her new husband before he bolted.

Shaking his acquisition until it jangled, Mason

beckoned her with a, "Your chariot awaits, princess."

Poor Mason. It seemed the time he spent in the dungeon had made him lose what little mind he owned. If she hadn't already vowed to never speak to her father again, this clinched it. Hopefully there was a cave, maybe with a nice stream and fish, for fallen bears. A place where someone would take care of him, nodding and smiling when he rambled on like a crazy creature.

"Why are you looking so glum, baby? I realize you're probably miffed we didn't get to cut our wedding cake, or dance the first song, but don't worry. I'll make up for it tonight when we get to the hotel."

"Excuse me? What are you blabbering about? There will be no hotel. We need to get to FUC headquarters as soon as possible and report in."

"I already did, princess, while getting ready for our big moment. Good thing your ex-fiancé was close to my size or I might have married you bare-chested. He's a decent bloke, that Eric, actually, once you get to know him. Of course, his cause was greatly improved by the fact that he stepped aside so you could be mine."

Her mind spun and for more than one reason. She decided to focus on the less traumatizing parts first. "Slow down and rewind. You called FUC?"

"Yup. Told Kloe what happened. As of now, you and I are off the grid. Consider yourself in my protective custody. I promise to do a better job this time."

"But the last time wasn't your fault."

He swiveled his head to stare at her a moment, the seriousness of his expression almost alarming.

"Yes it was. And it won't happen again. This time, I know what's going on."

"I'm almost afraid to ask, but what do you know?"

"Well, Gregory was most forthcoming—"

"Hold on a second. Who's Gregory?"

"He's the hyena who sent us the drugged cookies and tried to kidnap you. He was the mastermind's right hand man."

"You spoke with him?"

"Well, yeah, once he loosened up. Your dad thought it might be fun to throw the little bastard in with me when his henchmen couldn't get him to talk."

She pinched the bridge of her nose, a headache forming at his confusing tale. "And what convinced him to speak to you?"

"I don't know too many people who won't once you start eating them—while they're still wearing the limb."

It should have made her throw up. Yell in disgust. Cringe maybe even in fear. Instead, the image that crossed her mind of Mason gnawing on the hyena while he babbled his secrets...made her laugh. And more than laugh, she giggled, and howled, tears running down her cheeks so funny did she find it. Sure, it was kind of disturbing, but at the same time, seriously, who did that?

"Glad you're taking it so well. The guards weren't as impressed. Anyway, I got him to spill a bunch of secrets, which I've already relayed to FUC. Mostly stuff we already knew or guessed like how the mastermind was using shifters to extract DNA and then test serums on. It seems they achieved minor success in short-term enhancement in humans. However, temporary and permanent changes in shape-shifters, the mastermind's true goal, is still eluding them."

"Holy shit."

"Times a million," he agreed. "The one bummer is even with all we learned, Gregory couldn't give me an exact location to the new lab. He just kept saying, 'Who is God number one?' Whatever the fuck that's supposed to mean. But I'm sure someone will figure it out. Hint, hint, princess geek."

She stuck her tongue out at him, but couldn't help the warm pleasure coiling inside her that he thought she could solve the riddle the hyena gave them. "So who is the mastermind?" The question everyone had asked at one point or other during the investigation.

He shrugged. "Don't know. While Gregory knew a lot of shit, the one thing he couldn't tell me anything about was his boss. It's like he had some kind of mental block or something because his face would go slack jawed every time I asked. Kind of like when I asked him where the new lab was but minus the riddle."

"That sucks. We're no further ahead than we were then."

"Pessimist. We caught his right hand man. We escaped his clutches. I'd say we're miles ahead of the game and closing in at this point."

"If you say so."

"I do. Although, your dad was not so impressed at my methods of extracting info from the enemy. I had to listen to him yell while I dressed. Not for long, though, because I told him I'd eat him too. Sorry, but he really got on my nerves."

Jessie snickered. "No offense taken. I almost wished he'd kept goading you. Then maybe we wouldn't have gotten forced into this farce of a marriage."

"Is it really a farce? I mean, I like you, you like me. We're great together, especially when we get naked."

"Somehow, I don't think having sex once is the measure you should use," she replied dryly. *Even if he is right.* Sex with him went above and beyond her past experiences.

"Is that a challenge to have more sex? Yahoo!"

"No, that's not a challenge," she almost yelled. She tried to sound indignant; kind of hard, though, with her nipples pointing like beacons through her thin nightshirt and her pussy moistening enough to wet her panties.

One sniff was all he needed. "Ha. You are such a liar. Don't worry, my swan princess. We'll be at the hotel soon."

"With separate rooms. I am not sleeping with you again, Mason."

"But it's our wedding night."

Was he pouting? No way. She looked away lest she give in to his jutting lip—a lip she wanted to gnaw on. "It wasn't a real wedding. We can get it annulled, I'm sure, so long as we don't have sex."

"But I don't want it annulled," he growled.

"And I don't want a cheating husband." She blurted the words, the fear that kept her from caving in to his charm, without thinking.

He slammed on the brakes and swerved until they were parked on the side of the road. "I would never betray you like that, Jessie." He grabbed her hands and, when she wouldn't look at him, he forced her chin up so her eyes would meet his. "I know you think I'm some kind of playbear, but really, I've just been looking for the right woman. You. I was looking for you. And now that I've found you, I'm not going anywhere. You're stuck with me, princess."

"I don't believe you." But oh, how she wanted to.

"Then I'll prove it to you," he threatened, dragging her over the center console onto his lap.

She held up a hand to block his kiss. "How is making out going to prove anything?"

"Maybe if I make love to you a dozen times a day for the next fifty years you'll finally believe me when I say you're the one I want."

"But—" Okay, so she hoped he'd shut her up using his mouth. It worked. It also helped dispel for the moment her nagging worry that he just wanted her for a little while. He kissed her like a man enamored. A man out of control and desirous of her body. In other words, he seduced her with just his mouth and she took what he gave and begged for more, her hands clawing at his broad shoulders, frustrated at the material separating their skin.

A knock on the driver side window caused a rumbling groan to emerge from him, the vibration running through her frame from her perch on his lap. Embarrassed at her loss of control, she slid back over to her seat while Mason unrolled the window and dealt with the cop peering in at them.

While her *husband—oh God, that word freaks*

me out—talked the officer out of charging them with public indecency—the kind she wanted more of—she worked at cooling her ardor and reminding herself of the many reasons why getting involved with a bear was wrong. So very, very wrong, even if he made her feel…so very, very good. Dammit, why did the one man guaranteed to leave have to be the one who made her want to throw caution to the wind and do something reckless? Why couldn't she have enjoyed this level of arousal and intrigue with Eric? It would have made life so much easier.

Peeking over at his rugged countenance, she bit her tongue so as to not sigh because no logic in the world could explain why a playbear, of all things, made her feel every inch a woman. And not just a woman, a sexy, desirable creature with an insatiable need for him.

As they pulled away from the verge, she tried to pretend as if the last few minutes hadn't happened. He wanted nothing to do with that, or so she judged by the big hand on her thigh, her bare thigh because he pushed up the short material of her nightie to touch her flesh. She should have shoved his hand away. Okay, so she tried; he just wouldn't budge. The heat of his palm branded her skin and she couldn't help staring at the contrast of his hand on her skin. Ebony and ivory. What was the worst thing that could happen if she let him get between her thighs again? His tanned white flesh between her cocoa thighs, like a yummy Oreo, the kind with the extra thick white cream.

She moaned as she banged her forehead off the passenger window.

"What's wrong, baby?"

"Everything."

Scorching fingers crept up her thigh, causing her breath to hitch as one digit stroked the elastic edge of her panties. "Don't worry. We'll be at the hotel in a minute and I'll take care of you." As if sensing her coming rebuttal, he growled. "Don't make me pull over again. This time, cop or not, I won't stop until you're yanking my hair and screaming my name."

Oh, that caused a shiver to go through her. And truthfully, she was tired of fighting, and not just fighting him off, but her attraction to him. It wasn't as if she'd be sleeping with him with her eyes closed. She knew full well he was a womanizing playbear. It wouldn't last. But, in the meantime, why not discover more of the pleasure he could give? She was a modern woman with smarts enough to keep her emotions out of the equation. So why not have a little bit of fun?

Taking a page from Miranda's book, she decided to grab a bear by the balls, literally. Cupping him, she said huskily, "Stop talking and drive faster then." Hot damn, could that car move with the right incentive!

* * * *

Finding the nearest motel and checking in took an eternity, especially with a horny swan pressed against him, distracting him with her light touches and promising smiles.

When they finally made it to their room, he panted like he'd run a mile. Something of his exploding control must have shown in his expression because Jessie licked her lips, but she didn't back away. Oh no, his princess—*my wife*—peeled off her nightgown and stood there in just a simple pair of cotton panties.

He almost came in his pants like some inexperienced dweeb.

If he had to explain his extreme arousal, he would have said it was partly because of her smoking hot body, a good portion of love, but most of all, the awe and excitement of knowing that the woman before him—*my wife*—belonged to him. Whether she'd technically agreed or not, they'd gotten married. She was his. He was hers. And he couldn't have been happier.

No, wait. Once he got between her thighs for a taste, then he'd be happiest. Although, that might tie with sinking his cock inside her or...screw it. He'd do it all until he looked like a smiling idiot. *Or a bear in love.*

He tore his clothes in his haste to make it to her side, but she didn't notice, meeting him with a passion that made his heart swell. If he embraced her fiercely, her return kiss was even rougher. Demanding. She pushed him onto the bed, and he let himself fall, bouncing on the mattress. She regarded him for a moment, and he swelled under her gaze, his cock throbbing painfully.

Her hands went to her waist and she hooked her thumbs into her panties, pushing them down.

"Oh yes, baby," he sighed as she revealed a thatch of dark curls. "You are so beautiful."

"In your eyes maybe," she said deprecatingly as she crawled onto the bed.

For some reason, it bothered him. "You don't like your looks?"

On her hands and knees over him, the tip of

his cock straining toward her downy belly, she paused in her crawl and looked at him. "I like me just fine or else we probably wouldn't have any lights on in here. But just because I like my body doesn't mean that men find it attractive. I'm not exactly a petite girl."

"I know. You're perfect."

"Are you blind?" she asked, a puzzled crease lining her forehead. She pushed herself up until she sat on his belly, staring down at him. Talk about distracting, her moist pussy wet on his stomach.

Placing his hands on her waist, he let his thumbs stroke her soft skin. "I know what I see, and I see a beautiful woman with curves I want to lick and grope all day long." He slid his hands up to cup her full breasts. "I see a woman who enjoys her food and appears in fantastic health." He pulled her down toward him until her lips hovered just over his. "I see my wife. The most beautiful woman I could have ever imagined with the sweetest scent, the most tempting curves, and best of all, a sharp yet wicked mind."

Her breath fluttered over his mouth. "Oh, Mason."

"Yes?"

"You've already got me in bed naked with you, so instead of flattery, why don't you put that tongue to better use? Or was everything you've bragged about in the last month untrue?"

Did she just question his linguistic skills in the bedroom? Like hell. In a flash, he'd flipped her onto her back and nestled himself between her legs. To his everlasting joy, she let out a breathless giggle that quickly turned into a moan when he pressed his mouth against her inner thigh. Her citrusy scent enveloped him along with the heady aroma of her honey, the sign of her desire for him. He nuzzled her thigh before blowing softly on her sex.

She bucked. He grinned as he wrapped his arms under her thighs and hoisted her up while anchoring her. Time for some honey pie.

Using his long tongue, he licked her from the bottom edge of her cleft right up to her clit. Oh, that earned him a quiver. He did it again and again, languorous licks that made her moan and thrash while she begged him to get on with it and stop torturing her. He parted her lips and let himself probe her decadently hot channel, his sensitive tongue catching the tremble as her body reacted to his touch. Tasted her sweet honey, an ambrosia so sweet he closed his eyes lest they roll back in his head with pleasure.

While his tongue got intimately acquainted with her sex, he let his upper lip do its thing, his prehensile lip curling around her clit and tugging it. Oops, that made her come, hard and fast. Not that he stopped. Even as she screamed his name and tore out the hair in his scalp, he kept tongue fucking her as his mouth stroked her. He didn't let up even as the shudders kept coming in her body. He kept doing it until she screamed again, her second orgasm tightening her pussy around his tongue deliciously. So deliciously he couldn't wait any longer to have his cock inside her.

He positioned his body over hers, the tip of his dick probing at her. She should have been sated, but Jessie wrapped her legs around his flanks and squeezed. He went rocketing into her pussy, his prick entering her warm, wet haven, the quivers of her climaxes rippling up and down his length.

"Oh God, baby," he moaned, sinking deep and letting himself sit there for a moment.

"Fuck me, Mason," she whispered in his ear. "Fuck me hard," she begged. Then she bit his lobe hard.

God, he loved this woman. He jerked, his hips thrusting forward to butt against her womb. It felt so freaking good. He pumped again, and again. Her hands clawed at his back as she met him thrust for thrust. She moaned, "More!" over and over. So he gave it to her, feeling her channel tighten around him like a velvety fist. And when she spasmed into her third climax, he couldn't help following, bellowing her name, almost blacking out at the intensity of his orgasm.

He collapsed on top of her as all his muscles turned to mush. It occurred to him he should move, but as if she sensed his thought, her arms and legs squeezed him tighter. Her face nestled in the crook of his shoulder, her erratic breathing hot against his skin.

The moment was perfect. So right. He couldn't help himself. "I love you," he whispered.

She replied by pushing him off the bed.

Chapter Ten

"I love you."

He said those three words with absolute sincerity and for just a teensy tiny moment, she allowed herself to enjoy them. Then reality smacked her upside the head.

She shoved his unsuspecting carcass off her and onto the floor. Standing up on the mattress so that she towered over him, she planted her hands on her hips as she glared at him.

"What is wrong with you?" she yelled. "Why did you have to ruin it?"

"Me? Who pushes her husband out of bed after mind-blowing sex?"

"You're not my husband."

"Tell that to the priest who married us."

"It was a forced arrangement. We can get it annulled."

"Not likely. Your sticky thighs say otherwise."

She could only let out an inarticulate cry.

"Just so you know, that's not quite as hot as your yell when you come, and it still doesn't explain why I'm on the floor."

She took in a few deep breaths. They didn't calm her. "You said the 'L' word."

"Well excuse me for having feelings."

"You don't love me." An adamant claim even if a part of her wished he did.

"Hate to break it to you, but I do."

Panic fluttered inside as a part of her yearned to believe his words. The more rational part of her mind stomped on her heart's attempt at even going down that overly optimistic path. Like a proven manwhore could be believed. He probably said it to all the girls. She just didn't know why he waited until after the sex to use his deadly L-bomb. "Take it back!"

"Make me." He stood and glared at her, six foot something of bristling, naked male—and sporting an erection to boot. God, he looked so fucking hot—and irresistible. She fisted his hair and yanked his face in for a kiss, which turned into a rough embrace where they each vied for dominance.

He tackled her to the mattress, his heavy body atop hers, his knee spreading her thighs. He held himself off her, thinking to control the situation. She bit his lip, but he groaned at her aggressiveness, his tongue sweeping into her mouth to slide along hers.

She'd come three times already. She should have been good for months. Weeks at the very least, but at his evident desire, her body burned for more. Her clit throbbed for his touch. Her pussy quivered, wanting what only he could give her. She wished she had the ability to walk away from him. Wanted to deny his claim of love. Forget the forced marriage. But she couldn't fight the way he made her feel. How he made her body hum and made her scream in pleasure. He made her heart ache for something she thought she couldn't have. But, she could pretend for a few moments longer.

Pushing at his shoulders, she strove to regain some sort of control. He didn't budge. Her teeth latched onto his bottom lip and she bit him before she ordered, "Get on your back."

Almost instantly, he rolled onto his back. She sat astride him, the hot poker of his cock pressing against her backside. She cupped her breasts and pushed them together. He growled, his eyes, with their heavy lids, watching her intently. She bent forward until she dangled one breast in front of his mouth. He craned for the offering, his mouth latching on hotly, sucking her tender flesh, pulling a moan from her. Damn, but that felt good.

With him busy pleasuring her nipples, she hoisted her backside and hovered her cleft over his prick, gyrating just enough to rub the tip of it over her clit. She teased him, loving the slippery feel of his swollen head stroking over her sensitive clit. Apparently, he liked it a lot too. Large hands clasped her hips and, using his greater strength, he pushed her down onto his length, impaling her. And she loved it. She reared up on him, a low, throaty moan slipping past her lips, a moan matched by him as they both froze at the intense pleasure of their joining.

Bracing her palms onto his chest, she wiggled on him, the slow grind applying pressure on her clit. Her pussy tightened in response.

"Again," he panted.

She squirmed, swirling his dick inside, loving how he pulsed and stretched her channel. How it drove him wild. She did it again and again, their breathing harsh and erratic as their pleasure built. His fingers dug into her hips as he hissed "Yes" over and over. She sat on the cusp of bliss when, all of a sudden, the room moved as he rolled them so she lay beneath him. He managed to do it while never separating their bodies so he landed between her thighs, pistoning her. God, it felt so good.

Wrapping her legs around his flanks, she allowed it for a moment. Let him think he was in charge as he slammed into her willing flesh over and over. Just when his head went back, his eyes shutting as he strove for control, she knocked him sideways, the movement breaking them apart only for a moment before she climbed back atop his large body, sinking with a loud cry onto his cock.

She bounced on him while he moaned helplessly beneath her, his muscles straining as he strove to hold on. When he would have flipped them again, she growled, "Don't move."

He shuddered at her command. She rode him fast and hard, leaning forward to apply direct pressure on her clit, and to drive him even deeper. He lost it, his cock jerking inside her, flooding her with a wet heat. Seeing him submit to her, and even more arousing, losing control, took her over the edge. She rode her way to climax, the winner of the round for dominance. He got her back during round three in the shower when he took her against the tile.

Sated, finally, and too tired to speak, they fell into bed, spooned together like lovers. Or husband and wife. She woke to him making love to her, his body still cradled against hers, his cock sliding in to her welcoming heat from behind. What a way to greet the day.

While he never repeated the words—even during the spectacular angry sex—they hung between them. And Jessie didn't know what to do about it. It was one thing to suspect she felt something for Mason—feared she'd already lost her heart—another for him to admit he loved her. Not that she believed him. Sure, he acted like a man in love, caressing her body with a reverence not often seen outside of a church. But still…a bear and a swan? A womanizer and a geek? Talk about a recipe for temporary.

And what about the whole we're married thing? She knew she should confront him on what he intended to do about that. Fear held her back. What if he maintained that he loved her and wanted them to stay together? How long before she began to believe him and let her heart get involved? He would come across greener pastures soon—probably with blonde hair and a smaller ass—what would happen then? How could she allow herself to trust him knowing his reputation?

Inner dialogue arguing against it or not, it didn't stop her from having sex with him. It felt too good not to. But while sex was okay—and mind-blowing—talking about anything else, especially emotions, wasn't.

They traveled in that tense state of limbo for two days, driving a few hours at a time until she goaded him enough that he pulled off the road. Then, with a ferocity that excited her, he would make love her to like an animal, their grunting breaths steaming up the windows, their violent coupling rocking and shaking the car, abusing its poor shock absorbers.

During those moments, she didn't want to think of the future, nor even tomorrow. She just wanted to feel, sometimes pretend, that he truly did care and would never tire of her, never leave her. She hoped her weak desperation didn't show too much in her erotic assault of his body.

Dammit, what she wouldn't give for a gun so she could shoot herself for acting so emotionally confused. What happened to her cool composure? Her ability to shoot him down like a jet during war? Gone as soon as he quirked his lips and grabbed her.

At least their frequent stops for screaming climaxes made the drive pleasurable. As for their destination? He refused to tell her where they went other than to say she'd like it. Jerk. Nor would he say much more on what he'd learned from the hyena he'd eaten. The only thing she knew for sure was despite the hyena having met the mastermind, some kind of block—a mental kind—prevented the thug from telling them anything interesting about the sicko behind it all. He couldn't even provide a description. Or so Mason claimed.

It occurred to her more than once to wonder if Mason lied to her in a misplaced sense of duty, one he thought would keep her safe. But then again, did she really want to know more about the mad scientist who liked experimenting on her kind? Not if she wanted to sleep at night. Wait, she didn't sleep much at night anyway because of a certain lusty bear.

On day five, not even a half hour from their destination, according to him, they stopped and she piled out of the car, begging to stretch her legs and freshen up. Actually, she needed more than a stretch. She needed a good boink, as Miranda would call it. Knowing they'd soon end up cooped somewhere with other people, or so she assumed, meant this might be their last chance for intimacy. And much as she wanted to get away from Mason and his erotic touch, to try and regain her cool composure, at the same time, she dreaded it because she'd come to really enjoy his presence, and for more than just sex.

Bending over, she touched her toes in a mock stretch, wiggling her ass, a daring flirtatious maneuver that only he inspired. Never before had a man made her feel so desirable, so sexy. Under his obvious enjoyment of her curves, she blossomed into a sexual creature like she'd never imagined. Shaking her booty again, she smiled as she heard his rumble of interest. It might have had a lot to do with the fact she'd taken to wearing the skirts he bought her without panties. Apparently, his idea of outfitting her didn't include pants, which he claimed were a crime with a body like hers. So she retaliated to his unilateral command of her wardrobe by not wearing panties. It drove him nuts, in a good way. She loved the look in his eyes when he pulled up her skirt and saw her denuded cleft. It wasn't a look she thought she'd ever tire of. But despite the fun they kept having, still she worried the day would come when he'd lose his ardent gaze. When he'd wander away in search of new honey. The thought depressed her.

Straightening back up, she squeaked as his hands lifted up her skirt and cupped her bare bottom.

"Is that honey I smell for me?" he murmured in her ear before kissing her neck.

"Nope," she lied, her heart already starting to race

"You are such a tease, baby. Bend over for me. I want to taste."

"You wish. I'm not in the mood."

"Liar."

God, she loved their foreplay. "Prove it," she dared before taking off running. He chased her around the car a few times before he caught her. He hugged her tight as she panted, "I still don't want you."

Challenge thrown, and accepted, he just grabbed her around the waist and placed her on the car's hood. Pushing her knees apart, he inserted himself between her legs. Grabbing her hands, he held them in one big fist, restraining her, not that she resisted much. Flashing a cocky smile, he flipped her skirt up, revealing her pussy. She couldn't help the shudder that went through her when he stroked a finger across it, lingering on her sensitive clit.

"You know," he said in a conversational tone at odds with his smoldering gaze. "I used to think the best buried treats could be found in picnic baskets. Stolen ones, of course."

"Watched a lot of Yogi growing up, did you?" she said breathlessly as he sawed a finger in and out of her channel.

"Ah, Yogi. My hero. It was his cartoon adventures that sparked the picnic basket sniffing contest, you know."

"And you are the champion of said contest. I already know that. And your point would be?" She wiggled, hoping he'd give her the point—of his dick—instead.

He knelt and blew hot air on her exposed cleft. "Picnic baskets, while yummy, come a distant second to the honey between your legs."

A verbal reply on her part proved impossible unless her groaned moan of enjoyment counted. But he seemed to like her answer. He hoisted her buttocks and lapped at her, his abnormally agile tongue and mouth toying with her flesh, building her pleasure until she exploded, her climax a rippling affair that gripped him tight when he finally eased his cock into her.

"And this," he grunted as he pounded at her flesh, "is a hundred times better than finding a honeycomb."

"Freak," she panted before pulling him down for a scorching kiss.

It was as he pumped her, his hands on her hips, holding her lest she slide away from him on the slippery hood, that an amused voice interrupted their coitus.

"Son, how nice of you to bring a bird for dinner."

Shocked at having gotten caught—which she should have expected at one point given their public couplings—Jessie scrambled to cover herself while Mason fumbled with his pants as he tried to stuff his hard cock back in. Even more interesting, he turned red. A first. Nothing usually embarrassed him. But of greater concerns were the stranger's words.

"Mom, your timing sucks!" Her temporary husband whipped around in time for a bear hug that lifted him off the ground.

Oh shit. Jessie wished for a rock to hide under, although a hole in the ground would have worked too. Anything to hide from the embarrassment of getting caught screwing Mason, and by his mother of all people.

Speaking of whom, the elder sow released her son and turned a critical eye Jessie's way. She straightened her spine and met the gaze head on. As royalty, she knew how to appear dignified under any circumstance, even if she wanted to piss herself as the big bear—a matronly-looking type with the build of a lumberjack with breasts—looked her up and down then snuffled. Jessie found it hard to find a spot to look at because while nudity was a given in the shifter world, seeing her lover's mommy in the buff fell under the traumatizing category.

Jessie strove not to flinch when Mason's mother approached and sniffed her. "Swan?"

"Yes, ma'am," she replied.

"Don't call her ma'am," Mason interjected, throwing Jessie a wink that said, *don't worry, I've got this.* "We're married after all, so you should call her Mom."

The echoing yells directed at Mason, a duet of shock by her and her new mother-in-law, could probably be heard for several miles. And as for their identical cuffs upside Mason's head? His ears would probably ring for a few hours, which he totally deserved for dropping a bomb like that.

"Married? Don't you love your mother enough to invite her?" the sow huffed, her hurt plain to see.

"It was kind of spur of the moment," Mason replied with a sheepish shrug. "What can I say, the moment was just right and I just couldn't help myself."

"Don't lie to your mother," Jessie snapped. "My dad made him marry me. It was a shotgun wedding."

"Really," drawled his mother. "And may I ask why your father felt a need to bind you two?"

Jessie turned red as she tried to find a delicate way of saying her dad didn't appreciate her making out with bears.

"Her dad didn't like the fact I couldn't keep my hands off his daughter. Can you blame me? She's freakn' hot. And seeing as how I also happen to love her—"

Jessie smacked him. "What have I told you about using the 'L' word?"

"I'll use it if I want to. Love. Love. Lo-o-o-ve." He crooned the last one as he dodged swipes by Jessie while his mother looked on, probably wondering if they'd both gone insane.

He finally stopped taunting her, but being a smart man, hid behind his mother. Jessie glared at him and mouthed "Pussy." His reply? He stuck out his tongue and wiggled it. Jessie growled.

His mother shook her head, tsking. "Children, don't make me get the wooden spoon."

Mason kissed the top of his mom's head and muttered, "Sorry."

"I guess since you're married to the bird, that means I won't get to try out my recipe for swan soup," the elder bear said with a long-suffering sigh.

"Mom! I can't believe you said that. She's standing right there."

Jessie bit her lip so as to not laugh at his shock. Amusement that Jessie could see, but Mason couldn't, crossed his mother's face. "Impertinent cub. We'll discuss this further at the cabin." With those parting words, the matriarch shifted into her massive sow and lumbered off. Poor Mason, though. The danger had just begun.

Jessie went on the attack, pummeling his chest while yelling. "Are you out of your fucking mind? Why on earth did you bring me to your mother's?"

"Actually, both my parents live here."

"Whatever, you psycho bear. What possessed you to tell her about our temporary marriage?"

"It's not temporary."

"Yes it is."

"No, it isn't. And I will make you scream it's forever if you keep arguing. Do you really want to make me do that knowing my mother will probably return if we don't get to the cottage quickly?"

As threats went, it worked. She clamped her lips tight and climbed back in the car. But just because she wouldn't argue with him about it now didn't mean she wouldn't make him pay somehow later. Crazy gluing her thighs shut came to mind.

"So now what?" she finally asked through gritted teeth when he whistled without a care in the world, driving along the rutted dirt road bordered by vast trees.

"Now, we go stay with my parents and enjoy some good, old fashioned home cooking."

"I'm married to a mama's boy," she grumbled.

"Yup and proud of it. Chin up and smile, we're almost there."

"I'm going to kill you for this."

"Get in line, princess. Unless you want to tie me up and torture me. If that's the case, I'll bump you to the head of the line and supply a set of cuffs."

"Oh God, I think I'd rather face the mastermind," she moaned, banging her head off the glass again. Okay, maybe not, but now she couldn't stop imagining Mason in cuffs, naked and at her mercy. Damn, the things she could do to him. Her nipples tightened and moisture flooded her sex. And it was all his fault. Well, she refused to suffer alone.

"Oh Mason," she purred.

"What?" he asked absently as they pulled into a circular driveway paved in gravel outside a giant cottage that would have rivaled most hotel lodges for size.

"Speaking of cuffs, I can't wait to get you all tied up and lick my way down your chest to that fat cock of yours. I am dying to suck your great big prick while touching myself. And when you're throbbing hard and my pussy is slick and wet, I'm going to bend over and..." She never finished her sentence, hopping out of the car and smoothing down her skirt.

"Jessie!" he growled, following her. "You can't leave a man hanging like that. Come with me before Mom sees us. I know a place in the woods."

"Oh Mother, we're here!" sang Jessie, crossing her arms over her chest and throwing him a devilish smirk.

"Evil swan," he muttered, dropping his hands to cover his erection.

"I prefer orally gifted." She winked as she licked her lips, then giggled as she bent over and picked up the sunglasses she purposely dropped. His strangled moan was just the response she needed. Emboldened, she strode up to the cottage front door just as it flung open and a blonde whirlwind came flying out to bounce on her.

"Jessie!" Miranda's happy squeal just about rendered her deaf.

"Miranda? What the hell are you doing here?" she asked, staggering back from her enthusiastic hug.

"Well, after that attack by nasty old Cecile, Viktor decided to hide us in the safest place he could think of."

"How can bunking with Chase and Mason's parents be the safest place?"

"Because only an idiot would come between me and my first grandchild," said the sow she'd met earlier. "And I have a great recipe for idiots."

"Good to know. Although, knowing that, I'm surprised Mason made it through his childhood."

The three women turned to look at the rugged bear who grinned at them in oblivious pleasure.

"You and me both," muttered his mother. "I'm Kelly, by the way."

"Jessie," she replied, holding out her hand.

"Welcome to the family, Jessie." Tugged into a bear hug, she thought it best not to mention the temporary aspect of the relationship. Let the sleeping bear lie, or something like that.

And thus began the weirdest week of her life. Also the best one.

She met Mason's father that same day around dinnertime—which consisted of food enough for an army. The big man called Pete, who insisted she call him Papa Bear, hugged her so tight she probably went down a dress size. But she gained it back when she ate enough food—at everyone's insistence—to make her seriously wonder if they weren't trying to fatten her up for Christmas dinner. Over the next few days, she learned how a real family worked.

She learned to make cookies from scratch with Mason's mom and how to slap Mason's paw when he came to steal some. Needle and thread stopped being her nemesis. She spent her evenings playing board games, unable to stop her giggles when midway through every game, Chase accused Mason of cheating and took him outside for some brotherly love. Mason actually was cheating and even funnier, let his brother think he was bigger and badder than him during these bouts. Something that made her heart soften and Miranda snicker.

Papa Bear took to calling both her and Miranda daughter, bringing them treats every time he came home from work and cuffing the boys when they whined about not getting any. Papa Bear also gave the best hugs while Kelly's gruff yet doting demeanor showed her own affection. Jessie couldn't help loving Mason's parents. They were what she'd always wanted. What a shame she couldn't keep them.

Mason kept up their married charade, calling her wife at every opportunity no matter how many bruises she left on his shins. At night, she had to bite her cheek not to scream as he made her climax, usually two to three times before he rolled on to his back, dragging her in to snuggle at his side.

What a beautiful time. What a horrible charade. It made her want to cry.

And someone finally noticed.

Miranda dragged her into the backyard their third day there and handed her a gun. Jessie looked at it blankly.

"Are you suicidal?" she asked.

"Silly bird. Of course not. But I thought you might like to know how to shoot one in case the bad guys show up."

For the ditziest and bubbliest person Jessie knew, Miranda also doubled as the nicest and most thoughtful. "You really think I'll need to protect myself?"

"Nah. Mason would rather rip off his own arm

than see a hair on your head harmed."

"For now," Jessie replied gloomily.

"What do you mean for now? You're married. He'll always protect you."

"Didn't Chase tell you? Because I know Mason told him. My dad forced us to get hitched."

Peals of laughter rang out as Miranda, arms wrapped around her middle, gave in to mirth. "Oh, tell me you don't really think that?" She gasped in between giggles. "You have met Mason, right? Do you really think a room full of swans could force him to do anything he didn't want?"

Jessie frowned. "I guess not. But still, it's not like he had a choice unless he wanted to kill a few people."

"Trust me when I say Mason could have escaped if he wanted to. The man didn't. Doesn't that tell you something?"

"He's said he loves me," Jessie admitted.

"And?"

"The first time I pushed him out of bed and called him a liar and a whore." She at least had the grace to blush at her confession.

Miranda gaped at her. "Oh. Wow. And I thought Chase was difficult."

A frown knitted her brow. "Huh? I'm not following. Are you talking about Mason being stubborn about this whole fake marriage thing?"

"No. I'm talking about you trying to deny what you feel for him. Face it, buttercup, you love Mason."

"Do not."

"Do too."

"Do not."

"Don't make me shoot you," Miranda threatened, pointing the gun at her. "You love the bear and it scares the crap out of you."

Annoyance made Jessie's reply curt. "Well yeah, because chances are, once things blow over, he'll find some new ass to chase and I'll be left in the cold."

"Oh, Jessie, you poor misguided bird. I have news for you. Mason loves you. Did you know he's never, and I mean ever, spent the night with a girl before you?"

He hadn't? Her heart rate sped up. "How do you know that?"

"Because, like me, Mason has boundary issues and talks a lot more than he should about his private life. I also know he very rarely ever beds the same girl twice and never close together. And he's been with you what now? Over a week?"

"So? It's not like he's had many other women to choose from."

"He's never taken a girl to meet his parents."

"He did that to protect me."

Miranda aimed the gun again. "Stop denying it!" she shouted. "Say it!"

Was the psycho bunny in front of her right? Despite all her warnings to herself, did she love Mason? And could he truly love her back?

"I—"

"Go on. Say it. Say it, you cowardly bird."

"I—"

"Miranda! I bought you a carrot cake." Chase's bellow saw Miranda plucking the gun from Jessie's hand and holstering it along with hers before bouncing off, her face alight with hunger. But over her shoulder she tossed, "Live a little, Jessie. And trust a little. You might be surprised."

"What about our shooting lesson?"

"Are you nuts?" replied the bubbly blonde. "You with a gun? I'm not suicidal, you know."

No, but she knew one bunny whose computer would get a virus for screwing with her.

Or not.

After all, Miranda had given her food for thought and a good kick in the tail. Maybe she should lighten up and follow her heart for once. The worst that could happen was she'd end up with a broken heart, which she could technically blame on Miranda's advice. And if that happened, in the words of Elmer Fudd, *"It's wabbit season, and I'm hunting wabbits."*

* * * *

It shouldn't have surprised Mason that Jessie and his mother got along so well. How could they not when their greatest pastime was driving him nuts? At least their budding friendship, which kept them together part of each day, along with Miranda, relieved him of some of his worry. His mother would keep her safe. Because what Jessie didn't know was FUC was using them as bait, a little tidbit that almost saw Chase ripping his head from his shoulders for bringing danger Miranda's way. However, his brother's temper didn't worry him half as much as Jessie's reaction once she found out he fudged the truth.

He'd not told her everything Gregory had spilled. Like the fact their capture was always meant to be temporary. The mastermind wanted FUC to think Jessie and Mason were in danger, to hide them away, hopefully in the same place as Miranda and Chase. Apparently, while he and Jessie were out cold in transit, the hyena injected them with GPS trackers, then tipped off Jessie's father anonymously as to their location. Why it never occurred to him to ask the swan king how he knew where to find them made him want to slap his own forehead. At least Gregory, underestimating the swan guards, had gotten caught and spilled his secrets—along with his guts. Those Mason gave to the rats in the dungeons. He was more a thigh man himself.

Knowing about the bug, though, his first instinct was to locate and remove it. Kloe, when advised by phone, stayed his paw.

"This might be our only chance to snag them. Do you really want to spend the next few months or years always looking over your shoulder, worrying if they'll grab her?" Kloe's words resonated a little louder than he wanted. He didn't want to worry about Jessie getting captured. He wanted her safe. Worse, he knew Jessie would have volunteered if she knew. So why didn't he tell her?

Because he didn't want to see her frightened, constantly peering over her shoulder. Unlike Miranda, who could kick ass even as a human, Jessie was the brains of any operation. Give her a computer, she could demolish the enemy. Put her in front of a thug wielding a gun or claws and she was dinner. Not on his watch—well, unless he was the one feasting.

However, in order to keep his secret safe, he needed to not hover. She would have suspected something for sure otherwise. Knowing Viktor, and more of his buddies from the secret ops group he'd once belonged to, patrolled and hid in the acres of woods surrounding his childhood home helped, which was why he felt secure enough to bring Jessie to one of his favorite spots, the creek. With the weather abnormally warm for mid-November, it was probably their last chance to enjoy it until the spring.

"Oh how pretty," Jessie exclaimed upon seeing the bubbling water, immediately kicking off her shoes and wading into the creek. Still wearing the skirts he bought her instead of the slacks Miranda loaned her, she looked absolutely perfect and at ease in the sluggishly moving current.

"It's more than pretty," he said, pulling off his own shoes and rolling up his pants. He hung his shirt on a tree branch, a universal sign for his ops brothers that said, "I'm about to get busy so go away." He waded in, his toes squishing in the soft bottom. "It's where we're going to catch dinner for tonight."

"You brought me here to go fishing?" Incredulous eyes stared at him.

"If I say yes am I in trouble?" he asked meekly, now second guessing his decision. Fishing ranked in his top five favorite pastimes and he wanted to share that love with his wife. Or was this one of those things he should have kept for himself?

She laughed, a full-throated sound that sent shivers down his spine—the good kind that shot right into his cock. "I love fishing, but my dad forbade me from doing it when I turned twelve. Apparently, it was unseemly for a princess to catch her own dinner."

"It's also unseemly for you to ride me screaming 'Giddyup!' but that doesn't stop you," he replied with a grin. God, that image would probably remain burned in his mind as the most erotic sight ever. The only thing he could have added to make it even more perfect was a white Stetson. Thank God Christmas was just around the corner.

"Are you daring me to fish?" she asked, planting her hands on her hips, a cocky smile on her lips.

"Betcha I catch one first," he boasted.

"Ha." Quick as lightning, she bent over and stuck her face in the water. Seconds later, she straightened, a wiggling specimen between her full lips. She arched a brow.

"You are so fucking perfect," he groaned.

Tossing the fish onto the bank, she licked her lips and smiled. "Prove it."

Splashing through the shallow water, she dashed away, flinging clothes at him as she did until her ebony skin gleamed in the sunlight. She reached the deeper part of the creek and dove under, emerging several feet away with slick hair and water pearling on her skin. She swam back toward him with a saucy smile and stood when the water got shallow enough. A goddess rising from the waves and he needed to worship her. Or at least suck the droplet of water hanging from the tip of her nipple.

But his princess darted away from his grasp, her laughter dancing across the ripples in the water, tickling across his skin. He stopped chasing her and roared his frustration aloud. Not that she felt any pity for him. With a smirk, she headed back for the deeper depths and dove under the surface, the rounded curves of her buttocks flashing him before submerging.

While his disgruntlement seemed to amuse her, it brought him to the attention of others. From the brush alongside the creek, two sows waddled forth. They shifted as they walked, turning into the blonde twins, Eliza and Azalea. Think of a certain doll fabricated by Mattel and you had the lusty sisters who eyed him with interest.

"Mason!" Eliza squealed. "We've been dying to see you again."

"Screw seeing," her sister said with a lick of her lips. "What she means to say is we've not stopped thinking of you since last time. You were amazing."

"Um, thanks. But you see, I'm kind of—"

"Horny. We heard."

"We'll take care of that for you."

Actually, his dick had shriveled up to epically smaller proportions when they arrived. He just knew Jessie was watching, and probably simmering. This was bound to set him back in her eyes and reawaken her anxiety about her fear he would leave her for another. Or, could he use this to his advantage? "Sorry, ladies, while we had some great times in the past, I'm a married man now."

Laughter met his claim. "You are such a kidder," Azalea snorted, walking toward him with undulating hips.

"No joke. I met and married the most beautiful woman ever."

"Prettier than us?" Eliza asked, cupping her plentiful breasts. But not as full as his Jessie's.

"A million times, sorry. She's smart, too, and way too good for me."

The twins gaped at him. "You sound like you're in love."

"I am. And monogamous too. Sorry, but you'll have to let the others know I'm now a taken man and quite proud of it."

Seeing the blonde's eyes shift to something behind him, it didn't take him entirely by surprise when a slick arm slipped around his waist and a luscious pair of breasts pressed against his back.

"If you don't mind," he said with a grin, "the wife and I were about to get busy and would like some privacy." He didn't bother to watch the twins go, not with the growing wood between his legs. He turned toward Jessie and smiled down at her. "Hey, princess. I told you I'd catch you."

She snorted. "You and that tongue of yours are dangerous, and I'm not just talking about when you use it between my legs. I can't believe you turned them down."

"I can, because they're nothing compared to you. Don't you get it, Jessie? I love—"

Her eyes widened, and she shoved him to the side before he could finish. Stumbling in the water, he didn't see it, but heard the crack of a shot being fired. The more agonizing sound, though, was of Jessie grunting followed by the coppery scent of blood.

"Jessie! No!" His precious princess fell in the water, and he scooped her up, the hole in her upper shoulder bleeding and driving him insane. More shots came whizzing past, one narrowly missing his wife. Setting her down on a flat rock to keep her head above water, he lost his bearish mind. With a roar that sent the wildlife fleeing for its life, he changed in an instant and went charging in the direction of the shooter, or should he say shooters. The twins, wearing matching glazed expressions, each held a gun. Eliza, her arm jerking all over the place, fired

Eve Langlais

wildly, while Azalea, with better aim, still tried to hit him and Jessie, the bullets flying past uncomfortably close. Before he could reach them—and rip their heads off—Viktor came flying out of the brush and tackled them.

With the unexpected assassins incapacitated, he returned to Jessie's side and, changing shape first, cradled her in his arms.

"Oh baby, why would you push me out of the way like that? I would have taken that bullet for you. All of them, actually, to keep you safe."

Her lashes fluttered. "Why do you always get to be the hero?" she whispered.

"Because I love you, dammit."

"Yeah, well, I love you too, you giant furball." Even with the pain creasing her face, her lips curled into a ghost of a smile.

"You do?"

"Yeah. But don't let it make your head get any bigger than it already is."

Overjoyed, Mason kissed her temple, her cheeks, even the tip of her nose, murmuring, "I love you" over and over.

"Would you stop with the sappiness?" Viktor yelled from the riverbank. "I think I threw up in my own mouth."

"Want some crocodile boots?" Mason asked her as he carried her to the bank.

"A purse too," she replied before closing her eyes. The limpness of her body let him know she'd passed out.

Panicked, he didn't rip off Viktor's hand when the croc slapped a compress on the wound, applying pressure.

"Oh for fuck's sake, Mason," his old friend grumbled. "It went straight through, she'll be fine."

"Shut up. Wait until you find the one and she gets hurts. We'll see how brave you are then."

Viktor shuddered. "Never. I've seen what it did to you and Miranda. I prefer to keep my balls, thank you."

"You don't know what you're missing then," Mason replied, stroking Jessie's hair away from her face. "Now tell me why I shouldn't kill you for letting two shooters get close enough to hurt her in the first place. And what about Miranda and Chase? If we were attacked here, what's happening back at the cottage?"

"Yeah, well, we never suspected the sisters. They just came back from college and your mom swore they'd never betray them," Viktor sheepishly admitted.

"What, you didn't notice a pair of bears with guns?" Mason snapped.

"They didn't have them when they went wandering. After you talked to them, they started walking away only to stop and reach into a hole in some fallen log. Next thing we knew, the girls were shooting."

Mason didn't like the sound of that. It seemed too preplanned, but out of character at the same time. "The expressions on their faces reminded me of the hyena's when I asked him about the mastermind." A stoned look the twins still wore as other operatives, who'd arrived moments after the action, restrained them with cuffs.

"Like they've been brainwashed or hypnotized. As for your brother and Miranda, they're

147

Eve Langlais

safe. The ones that attacked the cottage were regular armed mercenaries, and humans to boot. We took them out easy and Miranda is unharmed, although Chase lost his mind and threatened to mow down the forest so no one can ever get that close again."

"Is it over, do you think?"

Viktor shrugged. "Doubtful. Until we get our hands on the mastermind, chances are none of us will be safe."

In that case then, I'll have to be extra vigilant with my wife. A need that ranked right up there with one to get her to repeat her words of before.

Chapter Eleven

Jessie stretched and winced at the tug in her shoulder. *I was shot.* Worse than her recollection of her injury, though, was the realization she told Mason she loved him. She groaned aloud.

"Hey, isn't that sound supposed to be reserved for when I'm touching you," the object of her thoughts complained.

She pried open one eye. "Go away."

"No."

"Please?"

He tilted his head as if to think about it. "Nope."

"I was delirious when I said it," she announced, going on the offensive.

"Liar. You love me. Not that I can blame you. I am, after all, pretty awesome."

"And conceited."

"Don't forget good-looking and an amazing lover."

"And annoying."

"Yes, and yet, you still love me." He laughed, then shouted, "She loves me!"

She scowled at him, even if her lips twitched. She stopped fighting the grin and let it blossom. "Fine. I care for your mangy carcass. What are you going to do about it?"

"Love you forever, of course," he replied in a matter-of-fact tone.

"Oh God, what have I gotten myself into."

"Nothing, but I can't wait to get into you." He waggled his brows suggestively, and it didn't surprise her to feel an answering tug below her waist.

"Okay, corny jokes and innuendos aside. What happened after I fainted like a girl?"

He crawled into bed before answering, sliding in beside her and pulling her into the circle of his arms. He relayed the events she'd missed, finishing with, "We put the twins through some serious deprogramming and all we could discover was that they attended some off campus party, which they don't remember, having gotten really drunk. We figure the suggestion to kill was planted then. As for the guns, no one knows how, when, or who planted them."

"And Miranda?"

"Is safe if going a little bonkers because Chase won't let her out of the house. But don't worry, she's making him pay for it in oral servitude. My brother is looking quite worn out already. I figure he'll let her out of confinement before the day is done."

"Will they be back? Do you think we can leave and hide from the mastermind and his minions?"

"No." And then he proceeded to tell her about the GPS tracking and use of her as bait. Something she already knew. But she appreciated his tardy honesty. Not that she let him know that.

"So let me get this straight, you lied to me. Dangled me like some tasty treat. And now can't even assure me that I won't get shot again."

His body tensed. "I know. It was wrong. I'm sorry. I—"

She laughed. Laughed until she almost cried. Shifting their positions until they were face to face, she smirked as he glared at her. "What's so funny, princess?"

"You. I already knew all that. You didn't really think Kloe would leave me in the dark, did you? I'm a FUC agent, Mason, and while it is kind of cute how you want to protect me, I knew when I took this job that there was danger involved. It doesn't scare me."

"What does?"

"Losing you," she whispered, suddenly stone cold serious.

Immediately, his gaze softened. "Never, Jessie. I love you. Every scowling, curvy inch."

"Prove it."

"But your shoulder?"

"Is fine. Now are you going to take care of me, or do I have to do it myself?"

As usual, her words goaded him into action. He kissed her gently, a sensual caress that stole her breath and made her heart swell. But she didn't want gentle. She wanted him to claim her, hard, fast, and sweaty.

Tugging on his hair, with fingers weaved through the silky strands, she opened her mouth and let her tongue slide into his, aggressively taking control of the embrace until his body, heavy and firm, pressed against her core. Back and forth they dueled for control of the kiss, their tongues sinuously sliding against each other, their teeth knocking as they tried to get closer. She tore her swollen lips from his and nipped his chin.

"I want you to mark me old style," she panted.

"For real?" His voice emerged thick with lust.

"Make me yours, Mason."

With a growl of need, he rolled off of her and yanked the sheets that separated them off before he flipped her onto her stomach. Hot kisses rained down her body from the top of her spine right down to the crevice of her cheeks. He hoisted her onto her knees and parted her thighs, his breath scorching hot against her cleft.

She closed her eyes and let out a whimper when he licked her, a slow, wet lick that ended at her clit. While he tongued her sensitive nub, his fingers parted her, sinking into her moist heat, and she couldn't help tightening around them.

He groaned. "God, you're so freakn' wet. I can't wait, baby. I need to sink inside you."

Good thing, because she was too close to coming as well. He positioned himself between her legs, the head of his cock probing her entrance. She rocked her hips back and sheathed him, loving how his fingers dug in to the flesh of her ass. He filled her up so perfectly. So fully. Slow and steady, he stroked her, his prick sliding in, then out, stretching her, pleasuring her until she mewled in need.

He increased his pace, the fleshy sound of their bodies slapping together louder even than their harsh breathing and grunts. He fisted his hand in her hair, the small tug of pain making her gasp then scream as she came, her channel rippling around his cock as he pummeled her willing flesh faster.

Fingers still twined in her hair, his other hand and arm wrapped around her waist, he guided her body up until his lips could touch the skin of her shoulder. Hips still pumping his throbbing hard cock into her, he bit her, pinching her skin until he broke the surface. When he sucked on his inflicted wound, while jetting his hot seed into her, it was like a thunderclap went off. While Jessie didn't believe in magic or weird esoteric forces, she couldn't deny she felt something in that moment, some odd sense of connection and rightness, followed by a whole of lot love. Of course, all those things could have been a delirious result of her second orgasm hitting, a whopper of a climax that shook her so hard her scream emerged silent, her mouth wide open, her body clenched.

In the aftermath of that, they could only collapse in heaving heaps, boneless ones. "Okay, that was pretty good," she admitted when she rediscovered the power of speech.

"Only pretty good?" he asked in disbelief.

She grinned at him. "Care to prove a swan wrong, bear?"

He did. A few times, actually. And she showed him how swans made the best cock gobblers, their ability to swallow things whole quite handy with dicks his size.

And then she died of embarrassment when the dinner conversation later that evening consisted of the merits in sound proofing guest bedrooms. But despite her red cheeks, sitting at a scarred wooden table made for giants, surrounded by Mason, his family, and Miranda, she'd never found herself happier. Or more loved.

A swan and her bear, no matter how incongruous, having a happily ever after. She'd have to take a picture and send it to her dad. He'd probably keel over. What fun.

Epilogue

The temptation waved back and forth, begged for it really. Due to the bad influence of one bear, Jessie couldn't resist. She wound up and slapped her husband's tempting ass. Then laughed as he bumped his head against the cabinet where he was currently buried under the sink.

"Not fair," he grumbled good-naturedly as he backed out. "I'm wearing too much clothing to truly enjoy that."

"And they need to stay on," she giggled as she placed her hands over his, which were already working at his belt buckle. Mason never liked to waste time when it came to making love to her. "Your brother and Miranda will be here any minute."

He blanched. "Are you insane?"

"Oh please. She's not that scary. She can't even change into her bunny anymore."

"That woman is dangerous, I tell you. Those pregnancy hormones have made her freakishly strong. Are you sure we have enough carrot cake to keep her happy? Maybe I should go out and buy a half dozen more."

"Calm down. I've got a pair of them already along with ice cream, pickles, cheese cake, and peanut butter."

"I still don't know why you invited them. Didn't we spend enough time with them up at my parents' place?"

"And I really enjoyed having another woman to talk to. So suck it up, baby bear, or you won't be getting any honey tonight."

"You're mean. And to think I was going to share my all-time favorite movie with you later."

"And which cinematic endeavor would that be?"

"Why *Batman Forever*, of course, with Val Kilmer, the most awesome Bruce Wayne ever."

"Val Kilmer," she murmured. The actor's name made some kind of bell ring, and she dove onto her laptop to type it in.

"Okay, I'm feeling a little jealous," her husband said, lifting her to sit on his lap. "And I swear if you're looking for naked pics of the guy, I might go a little rabid."

"There's only one hairy beast I like to see in the buff, so calm yourself down."

"Again with the foreplay. Cancel dinner. Let's play 'What's in your picnic basket?' again."

She ignored him—for now. They'd play naked later. "Aha!" Finding what she looked for, she leaned sideways so Mason could read the screen.

"I see a whole bunch of movie credits for a guy I personally don't think is that attractive."

"No one's as hot as you, now focus. What movie did Val Kilmer make in nineteen-ninety-six? Oh forget it, don't you see? *The Island Of Doctor Moreau*."

"What about it? Isn't that the mad scientist one where he experiments on people and animals?"

"Yes. I can't believe I didn't clue in before. I read the damned thing in college and saw the movie too. It's where the line 'Who is God number one?'

comes from. Remember, that thing Gregory the hyena told you? And guess what! There is a pharmaceutical company the next state over called…"

"Moreau Island Industries." Mason stood up, almost dumping her on the floor. He caught her and pulled her up for a hard kiss. "God I love it when you get all smart and geeky. Get naked while I make the call."

She grinned as he called the FUC office and let them know their target might lie within the Moreau Island facility. She stripped and bent over the couch as he barked out instructions for an immediate investigation.

Things since they'd returned from the boonies were going great. The shifter disappearances appeared to have stopped for the moment, not that Mason let her out of his sight. They'd moved into his condo and she totally enjoyed her father's shock when she announced they weren't getting divorced. The old bird thought he'd finally done the one thing to get her to tow the line and obey.

Ha. Like that would ever happen. She actually sent her dad a thank you card for forcing the shotgun wedding. Because of him, she'd found love, and she wasn't ever letting it go.

Even better, Mason took his promise of showing her his affection multiple times daily seriously. To her screaming enjoyment, of course. *And the swan princess lived happily ever after with her bear.*

* * * *

A week or so later, at Moreau Island Industries…

Viktor shot the lock off the last cell, already cringing at what he'd probably find inside. The other locked and dank rooms with their contents would haunt him forever, the occupants, pitiful experiments gone wrong, horribly wrong. Any semblance to humanity or sanity long gone. *The mastermind will pay for this.*

Jessie's deciphering of the clue ended up spot on with their furtive investigation of the premises showing large numbers of shifters and mercenaries disguised as guards. They mobilized their forces and struck within days of verification. And found a nightmare in the several levels of basements under the installation.

Viktor swung the final door in the macabre dungeon open, bracing himself. The lack of stench surprised him. All the other cells stank of waste and rot. Perhaps they'd cleaned this one out, their victim mercifully succumbing to the call of death.

A step into the room and at first he thought it empty until he caught a whisper of movement. Turning his head to the left, he watched as a huddled form in the corner lifted a head adorned with tangled red curls and eyes that glowed a bright golden. They blinked, and even though he couldn't see the face for the mess of hair, Viktor found himself enthralled with the luminous beauty of the orbs peering at him.

"Can you talk?" he asked when the female— had to be with those long lashes—kept staring at him. "It's okay. You're safe now. I've come to rescue you."

"Safe?" She spoke the word questioningly. Perhaps she didn't believe rescue had finally arrived.

"Yes, safe."

"Are you..." She paused, her soft voice fading. She scrambled to her feet, a dirty gown falling to her knees and molding to curves that raised her from his first impression of a child to woman. Viktor forced his gaze to her face with its delicate features. She lifted her pointed chin, some of her hair falling away from a grubby face with a pert nose and full lips. Staring him boldly in the eye, she said, "Are you my father?"

God he hoped not because that would make his body's response totally inappropriate. Sanity reaffirmed itself. "Of course I'm not your father. Don't you remember who you are?"

"I am Project X081."

He recoiled from the impersonal tag she used. "But what about before they began experimenting on you? What was your name then?"

A frown creased her brow. "Before? I was born here. Have always lived here."

The very idea appalled him. He held out his hand. "Come with me then and see what freedom is."

Slender fingers slipped into his and Viktor almost yanked his hand away as awareness of her slammed into him. He fought it as he led her back through the dungeon that housed so many failures and one sexy enigma. He let her tuck into him when they passed other agents as they searched the compound for clues.

Just before the exit to outside, Viktor stopped and said grandly, "Welcome to the real world." He flung the door open and let the sunshine in.

His mystery lady took one look at the vast green field, the blue sky, the sunshine. Then she turned and ran back the way they came, shrieking in terror.

* * * *

Damn FUC, and damn Gregory. The latter obviously betrayed their plans to the former and now everything was ruined. The shifter's special ops team overran the Moreau installation with guns blazing. The staff and guards put up a valiant if useless fight. With nowhere to escape and the enemy closing in, the mastermind did the only thing it could.

When the cell door opened fifteen minutes later, it was with big eyes brimming with tears that the mastermind murmured, "Oh thank you. Thank you for saving me." The fools bought it.

As they led the diminutive figure out to the waiting chopper along with those who could still walk, the plotting began anew, the devious cogs in the mind whirling, until a suspicious guard stared a moment too long.

Muah-ha-boo-hoo-boo-hoo. Wiping false tears, a grin threatened to burst free behind a tiny hand. So long as there was a breath to be taken, all was not yet lost.

The End (Not quite.)

Looking for more giggles, then check out the next story, **Croc and the Fox.**

Made in the USA
Lexington, KY
15 March 2018